SON OF A DESPERADO

William E. Vance was the author of radio plays, articles, and, beginning in 1952 with *The Branded Lawman* published by Ace Books, of some twenty Western novels. Living for much of his life in Seattle, Washington, in the 1960s he began writing hardcover Western novels, most notably *Outlaw Brand* (Avalon, 1964) and *Tracker* (Avalon, 1964), as well as *Son of a Desperado* for Ace Books in 1966, one of his most notable works. There followed a decade in which he published no Western fiction, only to return, publishing what remain his most outstanding novels with Doubleday: *Drifter's Gold* (1979), *Death Stalks The Cheyenne Trail* (1980), and *Law And Outlaw* (1982), his final novel. "Sound characterization, careful attention to historical background, and a fine story sense were Vance's strong points as a novelist," Bill Pronzini pointed out in *Twentieth Century Western Writers* (St. James Press, 1991). "Vance's untimely death cut short a promising career which seemed to improve with every book, and his works are well worth reading by anyone interested in the traditional Western story."

SON OF A DESPERADO

William E. Vance

GUNSMOKE

This hardback edition 2010
by BBC Audiobooks Ltd
by arrangement with
Golden West Literary Agency

ISBN 978 1 408 46268 3

British Library Cataloguing in Publication Data available.

Printed and bound in Great Britain by
CPI Antony Rowe, Chippenham and Eastbourne

I

OLD MAN RACKER's peevish voice came to the kid at the corral as he worked, smearing pine tar to the wire-cut on a gelding's leg. Harve straightened, wiped sweat from his forehead with one hand and stuffed the bottle in his hip pocket with the other. He slapped the gelding's flank and climbed the corral fence and dropped to the ground.

"Grouchy ol' devil," he murmured and hurried toward the ramshackle unpainted board house on the rise. The house seemed to lean against the eternal wind that blew mostly out of the southwest.

"Harve!" The self-pity of a sick man was in the call. Then, plaintively, "Where in tarnation is that rascal, anyway?"

"Right here, Mr. Racker," the kid said and stepped up on the porch, blinking his eyes against the gloom that held wherever the sun couldn't reach. "You wanted something?"

"Forget you're going to town today?" Racker sat hunched in his chair, a quilt around his shoulders. The brown of his

5

face had paled out a sickly yellow since he'd hurt his kidneys in a fall and couldn't get out in the sun any more.

"You didn't tell me," Harve said and he came on into the room and took the bow-backed chair beside the fireless fireplace, across from Racker. He put his elbows on his knees and stared at his clasped hands.

"The devil I didn't," Racker said with the crossness of a man whose life is bounded by four walls. "Told you a week ago."

Harve didn't argue. That's how it'd been for a year now, ever since the old man hurt his back. Forgetful he was, among other things. Sometimes, Harve didn't think he could stick it out. Racker was just too blame hard to get along with. But he knew he would. He'd thought about it before, but he knew he'd feel guilty if he gave in to the urge to saddle up and shake loose from this range. "I guess I forgot," Harve said quietly.

Racker flicked a look at him. "Maybe I just thought I told you," he said less sharply. "The note's due, Harve, and you got to pay it off." He brought out a money belt from under the quilt and laid it across his knees. "Not enough here, so you'll have to take that string you just broke. Take 'em in and sell 'em."

Harve felt a pang at this news. He hated to sell the horses he broke. He knew it had to be done when you're working a horse ranch, but every single one of the animals he'd gentled, taught to neck-rein and other refinements of a well-trained saddle horse meant something more to him than just a piece of horseflesh. Even the prospect of a period away from the quarrelsome demands of Burt Racker didn't raise his spirit. Not too much, anyway.

"How much you want for them?" he asked.

"Make the best deal you can," Racker said and then added warningly: "But don't go giving them away."

"I'll bargain," Harve said, his spirits beginning to lift. The mere thought of a valuable bunch of horses being entrusted

6

to his care made him feel important. And to get away from Racker, just for a little while; he felt the need of it.

"Don't try to be too sharp, though," Racker amended crossly. "Or you might have to drive 'em back."

"All right."

"Another thing, Harve: you got to get enough out of them to make up the difference 'tween what I got here in the money belt and what it takes to pay the note."

"How much is that?" Harve asked.

"Dunno. Mr. Purvis at the bank will figure it for you."

"What'll I do with them horses while he figures?"

Racker's forehead wrinkled. "Most likely thing is put 'em in Fedder's corral. Shouldn't charge more than two bits a head. Don't let him sting you, boy. He will if he gets half a chance."

"He won't sting me," Harve said confidently.

Racker tilted his head to one side. He was silent, looking at the kid and then at the money belt. "You been a good boy, Harvey. Maybe one of these days we'll make a partnership. Go fifty-fifty: my spread, your work. . . . Now shake a leg."

At Racker's "proposition," bitterness again crept into Harve's thoughts like a taste of wormwood. *Like the saddle the old man had promised. And the raise in pay. He's keeping me on here with lowdown promises he doesn't mean to keep, not ever . . .* "I'll fix everything handy before I leave," he said, trying not to sound balky. He got to his feet and headed toward the door.

"Harve."

Harvey stopped in midstride.

"I'm hard to get along with," Racker said, a contrite undertone in his voice. "I know it, boy. But I'm stuck here in this blamed chair and it riles me something fierce. Just be patient, Harve, and you won't be sorry."

There it was again, always that almost-promise. "Yes, sir," he said, and went on out.

He split kindling, carried in firewood and filled the water

bucket. He put everything in easy reach for Racker and then went out to get the horses ready for the trail.

Harve took his frustration out on the horses. He cursed them wholelheartedly and jerked on the lead ropes to get them in place; then he was remorseful and gave all of them a small measure of grain, looking at the house to make sure Racker wasn't watching from the window. A mean-souled man, this Racker, but Harve could get along with him except when he was hurting; and he let Harve do pretty much as he pleased, long as the work got done.

In the shack he lived in, close to the barn, Harvey Holley dressed in his town clothes, swearing because he was growing so fast the pants leg cut him above the ankles. His newest shirt had shrunk too, or else his dad-gum arms were growing faster than anything else. He tied a purple scarf around his neck, settled the Stetson on the front of his head and then cuffed it back and went out the door and slammed it shut. He stood there for a minute, looking at the horses bunched in the little corral, feeling pride in them because he'd broken every one of them himself. He bow-legged on up to the house.

Silently, almost grudgingly, Racker gave him the money belt and a list of supplies, written on brown paper that had been torn raggedly from the cover a mail-order catalog had arrived in. "Don't take no more time than needful," he warned, his voice sharp and complaining. "Me all alone and no tellin' when I might be took."

"All right," Harve said stolidly, keeping back an impulse to say something nasty.

"And keep out o' Frobacker's poolroom and the Grand Central Bar," Racker went on, "ain't no fit place for a kid."

A kid, Harve thought, *far as that stuff is concerned, but not when it's work to be done. I'm a man, then.* He said, "Don't worry, Mr. Racker, I'll be right back, fast as I can." He talked as he put the belt under his shirt, next to his skin. He stuffed his shirttails back inside his pants. "Don't you worry none, Mr. Racker."

8

Racker's face loosened for a moment. He said, "You've been a good worker, Harve. I won't forget."

Harve stamped out the door, Racker's words leaving him cold. He'd heard them too many times. Praise, when Racker wanted something done in a hurry and done right. And fretful complaint the rest of the time. *Don't know why I just don't light out and not come back,* Harvey thought, as he swung up on his roan, picked up the lead rope and began the long trip into Rowel.

Harvey Holley was eighteen that summer, leather-lean and tough as rawhide. He could ride and rope with the best of them and knowing it, he didn't get a big head; neither did he try to throw his weight around. He was what the ranchers out in that part of the country called a good, decent kid, hard-working and dependable. He was the driving force that kept the Double H going, the workhorse that put Racker's spread in the top bracket so far as diversity—beef and horses—and good range management were concerned. The qualities that made Harvey Holley into the kind of man he was rapidly becoming, were also the qualities that kept him from abandoning Racker.

Coming out of Chinch Pin Draw, Holley saw a small band of Rappys, the peace-loving but fierce Araphoe, camped by the springs. He slowed his roan without thinking. The Rappys were friendly enough but they were always short of horses. He kept his herd moving along at the slower pace, seeing that all movement around the springs had ceased as they watched his approach.

He worriedly wished he could swing out and around and pass them at a distance but his unknown pride kept him from it.

Just don't say nothing, he reminded himself, and kept right on going. *Can water the remuda at Pipestem Springs.* He touched the roan with a spur, resuming his normal pace.

The Indians were a shoddy-looking bunch, seven braves, three squaws and several little ones. They all stood still, looking at him as he came steadily onward. He noticed they didn't have enough horses to go around and felt another twinge. He tried to comfort himself with the thought that he couldn't remember when there'd been Indian trouble. But this bunch looked hungry. No telling what an Indian would do when the kids got to whining for something to eat.

He touched the Colt on his hip and felt reassured for a moment. His moment of reassurance faded as the biggest one of the braves moved out to intercept him. His throat felt kind of choked up and he tried in vain to relax his tightening stomach muscles.

II

THE DOUBLE H outfit bore the print of Harvey Holley's hard-working hands. It was different from most of the ranches in the long, wide valley that started small at Star Gap on the north, and ended small at Rowel on the south; it was a contradiction in its weather-tight buildings and well-tended fences, and the shabby living quarters. Its buildings sprawled on a rise where the valley narrowed in for a spell before spreading out again; the valley itself was like an hourglass. The frame house was the only blotch on the landscape, other than Harvey's lean-to, and that's how Racker wanted it. He wanted to appear poor. A casual rider coming on the ranch proper would conclude that here was a kind of run-down, rawhide and baling wire kind of spread. That illusion was exactly the one Racker wanted to convey.

He thought about this moodily as he watched Harvey out of sight beyond the nearest ridge. He sighed deeply and got painfully out of his chair and walked stiffly to the old oak wardrobe and opened a door. He searched for and found a bottle, uncorked it, drank sparingly and replaced the cork and the bottle, shut the door and wiped his mouth with the back of his hand. He made his slow, unsteady way back to the chair and was lowering himself into it when he saw the rider on the black horse crest the near ridge to the north. Racker stood there, half-in and half-out of the chair, looking hard, his heart beating a little heavier, like it always did when a stranger came riding by.

He pushed the chair to the open door and resumed his seat, pulling the quilt carefully over the .44 Colt resting between his legs. He kept his fingers curled around the butt of the gun, deriving some small comfort from the feel of it, waiting.

The rider came on past the log barn and pole corral without slowing. He was a big, dark man with a handsome black mustache. He stepped from the back of a big black gelding without a single mark of white, nodding to Racker in a pleasant manner while he loosened his cinches.

Racker called from the doorway, forcing a note of welcomme in his voice. "Howdy, mister. Light a spell and rest your saddle."

The red-lipped man grinned at him and leisurely walked up on the porch. He stopped under the edge of the roof and leaned the point of his shoulder indolently against the weathered four-by-four that helped support the roof. He kept his bright searching black eyes on Racker, an amused smile on his lips.

"Where's the boy?" he asked, without answering Racker's unnecessary invitation.

Racker swallowed hard, his Adam's apple working, while a visible shudder momentarily shook him. "What boy?" he asked in a croaking whisper.

The tall man shrugged. "It's been a long time, but I waited over there in that clump of cedar on top the ridge while Hack rode in with the boy. Hack had it all set up beforehand. He come back satisfied that he'd done the right thing." The man laughed. "He got himself killed a little bit after that and I spent some time in the pen. But I always wondered how it worked out. And bein' in the neighborhood, I thought I'd find out."

"Nobody around here knows he's Hack Holley's kid," Racker said in a dry, rasping voice.

"I asked where he is," the stranger said, his stare hardening, settling on Racker with a piercing intensity.

"Now, looky here, mister—"

"No, you look here," the stranger said, stepping away from the porch post. "Hack brought the kid here. He gave you all the gold we had between us—yeah, and a ranch, free and clear. Hack might be nothing but dust now but he just might be wondering what happened to his kid. I'm a voice from the dead, you might say." He smiled as he spoke but there was nothing reassuring in his smile.

"Takes a heap to raise a kid," Racker said in an almost inaudible tone. "It takes a sight o' money and everything else."

The man's smile deepened without changing anything. "How many riders you got, old man? he asked, in that smooth, soft voice. "How many men on your payroll?"

Racker's eyes were on the quilt that covered his knees. He wondered if he could cock the pistol and get it out in time. Maybe he could fire through the quilt. This was a moment he'd lived over, again and again, a product of guilty years. Now that the moment he'd dreaded was here he didn't feel up to taking care of it. His thumb curled over the Colt's hammer and then he stopped all movement as the big bore of the stranger's gun looked him in the eye.

"Don't bat an eyeball, old man," the stranger said, and stepped forward and jerked the quilt aside. He lifted the gun from Racker's unresisting hand and threw it out on the ground. The big black shied and then sniffed at the gun.

"I—I—" Racker faltered, then with a gasp quit trying to talk.

"Yeah, I know. You didn't mean to use it." The man stepped back, holstering his pistol. "I'm still waiting for an answer, old man. Where's the boy? Did you do away with him?"

Racker paled and swallowed hard. " 'Course I didn't," he said indignantly. "He rode into Rowel with a bunch o' horses. Had to meet a note, yeah, and had to sell horses to pay it

12

off." His voice ended on a piteous note, begging for sympathy.

The man didn't respond any more than a snubbing post. He stared at Racker without any outward show of emotion and this Racker found more terrifying than if the stranger had ranted and raved. "What'd you do with all that gold Hack left here?"

Racker put his hands together in supplication. "Listen, man, it takes money to live. All these years I been keepin' that kid and the gold is all gone. I swear it. Why else would I sell my horses to pay off a note?"

"You probably got good reasons, old man," the stranger said, pleasantly enough. He half-turned away and spoke again. "I'll look him up. Maybe I can get more truth from the kid than I can from you."

"Who are you? What're you doin' here?" Racker shrilled. "What'd you come back here for, anyhow? You ain't needed." The mere fact that the man was leaving gave Racker a piece of his nerve back.

"That kid's daddy was my friend, old man. Know what the word friend means? I guess not. Well, I'm checking up on how the plans Hack had for his kid panned out. That's who I am and that's what I'm doing here."

"He's a good boy," Racker said. "He works hard and he knows the worth of a dollar."

The stranger didn't reply as he was tightening his cinches. He mounted the rangy black and sat there for a moment, staring at Racker. He said, finally, "I'll talk to the boy. I might be back to see you."

"I'll be here if you do," Racker said miserably. "I ain't able to ride. I'm a sick man, mister, mighty sick."

The man stared at Racker for a long moment and then turned his horse and rode south at an easy lope.

Harve could see the wrinkles on the chief's face. Harve knew he must be the chief because he was the only one with a feather, a single eagle's feather, dyed a brilliant red, worked somehow into the black braid on the left side.

Harve could see expectancy in all of them. He cursed himself for being too prideful to make a wide circle around them. Too late now, to make a fight of it; anyway, this was not a good place. Maybe it wasn't too late to run. None of the grass-fed Indian ponies could keep up for long with his Double H horses. He was set to dig in his spurs when the chief raised his hand, making the peace sign.

Harve rode on, somewhat reassured, but still uneasy. The horses grew nervous from the smell of the Indians and one of the snorty ones near bolted. Harve had a few minutes trouble regaining control. He finally got them quieted down and the chief raised his hand again.

"Me Red Eagle. You got food, white boy?"

Harve studied the unfathomable face with its lines of age and it told him nothing. The gaunt ribs on the brave told him more. Harve nodded. "A little, Red Eagle."

Red Eagle waved his hand toward his silent people. "No meat in our lodge."

Hell, Harve thought, *they don't even have a lodge*; but he listened politely.

"The hunting is no good. Our bellies are empty." He gestured widely. "The agent said there is nothing from the Great White Father this moon, nor for many more."

In a vague way, Harve knew the red tape got tangled. He had a little bacon in his saddle bags, some rice and a couple of cans of tomatoes. Not enough to feed this bunch. What he had would only whet their appetite. Anyway, he told himself, he wasn't responsible for them. He looked at the sky, saw the buzzards wheeling high above, pinpoints a-gainst the blue; and felt a crawly sensation in his spine. He muttered, "We'll see."

As he dismounted a sage hen scuttered through the brush. Harve whipped out his gun and fired and almost hit one of the little ones rushing after the hen with an upraised stick. It was a luck shot, knocking the hen down, where it flopped. The Indian kid dropped his stick, grabbed the hen and brought it back, holding it by its feet. The head was gone. Red

14

Eagle looked at Harve in admiration as he loaded his gun. *It was a dad-gummed lucky shot,* Harve thought. He'd never hit a sage hen on the run before.

Red Eagle spoke gravely. "Good omen," he said. "The hunting will be better."

Harve sure hoped it would before this bunch started butchering beef in the hide. That could cause trouble around here. The ranchers were real spooky about getting their beef taken by rustlers, Indian or white.

He opened his bags while the women hastily started a fire smoking. He dropped the bags on the ground while he tethered the horses a distance from the springs. The Indians stood around the saddle bags, looking at them, but didn't touch them. Harve came back and picked up his bags and carried them to the fire. The sage hen had already been plucked and dropped into the cooking pot. Harve felt sick for a moment; they hadn't even cleaned the bird.

He dumped what rice he had in the pot and placed the bacon and canned stuff on the ground. He said, "Okay, Chief. That's about the size of my help. Wish I could do more but I'm just one lonesome cowpoke and that's it."

Red Eagle didn't fully understand but he recognized a friendly act. He put his hand briefly on Harve's shoulder.

Then they forgot about him as they gathered around the cooking pot, looking at it in a way that made Harve wince. He didn't lose any time tightening his cinches and getting the string to moving again. He looked back as he topped the next ridge. The Indians were digging into the pot. He knew the meat wasn't done, was still raw. *Sure a hungry bunch,* he thought, and felt unhappy about them. *What the hell can I do?* he asked himself in self-disgust. *Ought to feel lucky they didn't try to take my horses—and the money belt.*

At Pipestem Springs, he let the horses drink. They were crowding the soft mud bank, when a rider came up out of the arroyo, appearing out of nowhere, it seemed to Harve, who was startled for a moment. He relaxed his hand from his gun, when the rider appeared so unconcerned about him. Carrying the money and responsibility for the remuda had made Harve nervous.

Harve managed a rueful grin as the man put his fine-looking black, lathered and sweaty, down to the water's edge, looking Harve's string over as his horse drank thirstily. He took off his hat and used a handkerchief to mop his brown forehead. He replaced his hat, put the handkerchief away and got down from his horse, walking upstream to a clear spot, where he knelt and drank. He rose in a supple movement and walked back, wiping his black mustache, first one side and then the other, giving the ends a twist, and miraculously imparting a neat spike. A wide grin split his darkly handsome face as he looked at Harve.

"That horse of yours sure been used," Harve said bluntly, his indignation rising. He hated to see a horse mistreated, or any animal for that matter.

The stranger shook his head contritely. "That he has. Good thing he's the horse he is. Nice lookin' bunch you got."

Harvey's resentment vanished in a flash in the warmth of that smile and those words. He nodded. "Best in these parts."

The big, dark man glanced from the kid back to the horses. "Takin' 'em to town?"

Harvey nodded importantly. "Yes, sir. All by my lonesome."

"Should bring a fair price. Better than average, I'd say."

"You sure know horses," Harve said, flushing at the left-handed compliments he was trading with the stranger.

"Some. You raise these?"

Harve nodded. "An' broke every one myself." He added with pride: "These are practically all hand-raised. But not pets. Just good stock."

"Fine job you've done," the stranger declared, admiration filling his eyes and tinging his speech. "Got a spread, I reckon? All your own?"

"Well, not exactly," Harvey said and cleared his throat and shifted in his saddle. "I work for old man Racker. Run

16

his spread for him. He's all crippled up and can't get around much."

"Hum, that's too bad. He's lucky to have someone like you to look out for things just like they belonged to you. Real lucky." He moved to his horse, unloosened the girth and straightened the blanket. He ran his hands down the handsome black's forelegs, massaging them and, that finished, he leaned against the horse, building a cigarette.

Unconsciously, Harvey reached for his own tobacco sack. He built himself a smoke and got it lighted and then slid to the ground and unloosened his own cinches and straightened his saddle blanket and tightened the cinch straps. He hitched at his belt and said, "Stranger around here, ain't you?"

The big dark man laughed, showing a wide expanse of white teeth beneath his black mustache. "Yeah. Ridin' through. Name of Waldrip. Price Waldrip." He swaggered over and offered his hand.

Harvey Holley felt a pleasurable warmth for the big man as he shook hands. "Glad to meet you," he said and gathered up his reins. "Got to get these horses movin'. Old man Racker all alone at the ranch 'til I get back."

"I'll ride along with you," Price Waldrip offered and was sitting his saddle waiting, as Harve gathered his lead ropes.

Waldrip was an entertaining talker when he wasn't listening to the kid. Harve had the uncomfortable feeling, as they neared the overnight campsite, that he'd done too much talking and not enough listening. He'd stretched the truth in a place or two and built himself up to be a pretty handy man to have around. Reviewing it all in his mind, he decided it'd be all right. After all, living with a man like Racker, a fella had to do something to get rid of the feeling he was useless as warts on a bull's nose, which was the line Racker used from morning to night, day in and day out.

But this fellow Price Waldrip had been lots of places, one could tell. He'd topped many a hill and crossed plenty

17

creek water. He knew his way around. Harve knew a good man when he saw one. A mighty fine man, Waldrip.

They pulled in at an old camp ground beside the creek at sundown and stopped the horses.

Waldrip looked the surrounding country over carefully. "Now see here, Harve," he said, "let's fill our canteens and push your remuda up that there gulley above the creek. Nothin' here for them fine hosses to graze on."

"Sounds good to me," Harve answered promptly and dismounted to fill the canteens.

Waldrip sat his horse, watching, and building a cigarette. He scratched a match on his saddle horn and lighted his cigarette. When Harve finished his own canteen, Waldrip tossed his own. By the time the last canteen was filled, the horses had finished drinking.

Harve mounted and got his string moving up the little valley through which the creek meandered. At the first turn, Waldrip sat his horse and surveyed the country from higher ground. Then he rode on up ahead of Harve and selected the spot where they'd camp for the night.

Waldrip was a handy man around a camp. In no time at all, while Harve put the remuda on a picket line, Waldrip gathered wood and got a small, hot fire going and the frying pan warming. When Harve finished his work and came to the campfire, Waldrip had a pot of water on for coffee.

"We'll just put what we got together," Waldrip said casually. "No matter we eat everything we got. We'll get breakfast in Rowel, by doggy."

Harve's face fell. "Golly, I gave everything I had to them starving Indians at Chinch Pin Springs."

Price Waldrip's black eyes glinted. "You *give* it to 'em?" in an unbelieving voice. "You mean you just plain give it, no barter, no nothin'?"

Harve swallowed. "Yep, reckon I did. They's about the hungriest lookin' bunch I ever run across."

Waldrip leaned over and hit Harve lightly on the shoulder. "Don't take on about it," he said, in a bright and cheerful manner. "I reckon it shows your heart's in the right place. But givin' an Injun anything is a big mistake. That's because the Injun takes it as a sign o' weakness in a man. Come dark they just might come after your remuda." He glanced at the horses grazing on the picket line. "That'd be a shame, a dirty shame to lose them hosses, Harve."

"It'd be worse that that," Harve said worriedly. "Guess I won't do much sleepin' tonight."

Waldrip laughed heartily. "Don't let it curb you none, boy," he said. "I always sleep with one ear and one eye open. Anyway, they don't find us camped down at the crossin' they'll figure we ridin' straight through without stoppin'."

The meal Waldrip whipped up was as good as any Harve had ever tasted. *Mayby,* he thought, *that's because I been doing all the cooking at the Double H, since just about as long as I can remember.*

After the supper gear was cleared away, Waldrip spread a sougan close to the fire and dropped back on his elbows, all the marks of a man about to talk. And Harve's blue eyes gleamed, as he waited for the man to tell him what was across the mountains.

Disappointingly, Waldrip asked, "How old are are you, Harve?"

"Well, 'bout eighteen, I reckon," Harve said without much enthusiasm.

"Don't you know for certain?" Waldrip insisted.

Harve shook his head.

"Old man Racker—he your kin?"

"Not that I know about."

"How'd you come to get there, then?"

"Well, I don't rightly know, Price," Harve said. He didn't much want to talk about it. Not that he hadn't given the matter a lot of thought, but that was strictly in his mind. But Price had been mighty nice. No harm in talking about it. Come a few days and Price would be across that next hill and that'd be the end of it. "I come to Racker's when I was 'bout four or five. That'd be, let's see, some fourteen years ago, this last spring."

"Next spring," Price said.

Harve stared. "What'd you say?"

"I said maybe next spring," Waldrip answered, smiling his red-lipped smile. "Go on, boy."

"Not much to go on about," Harve said. "I remember riding with my Pap. He held me on the saddle in front of him. He had on a corduroy coat, I remember, and it was kind of rough and smelled like tobacco an'—an', I don't know, maybe sagebrush or pineneedles or something. He handed me down to Racker. I was real little, Price, and I don't remember much about it. And Racker never did say much except that a man got rid of what he didn't want."

Waldrip sat up and violently threw his cigarette into the campfire. "That was a hell of a thing for him to say," he said in a voice that was surprisingly mild.

Harve chuckled. "Oh, I don't know. Racker's a man who's had his troubles. His bark's worse'n his bite, any old day." He felt moved to defend Racker for some inexplicable reason, adding: "He's got his good points, Price."

"Only thing is you don't know what they are," Waldrip observed and began his preparations for sleeping.

The night had turned chill, with a strong wind brushing through the draw, rattling the brush. They crawled into their beds and Harve snuggled down deep under his blankets, using his saddle for a pillow. With the pleasant sound of the horses grazing he fell asleep.

It seemed almost instantly he awakened, with all his senses alert. He looked at the sky without turning his head, with the tip of his nose hooked on the edge of the blanket. He located the Big Dipper without trouble and estimated the time as past mildnight. He waited again for the sound that had awakened him. It came in a faint whisper from the other side of the dead campfire.

"Harve!"

"Yeah," Harve whispered an answer.

"Did you hear it?"

"What?" asked Harve.

"Dunno. Something movin' down by the crossin'. Them Injuns, I'll bet."

Harve turned his head slightly, aiming his ears toward the crossing and cupping them with his hands. The wind had died away to nothing. Silence bore down on them and it seemed colder than when he bedded down. He heard the slight sound of the horses grazing up the draw; other than that, nothing at all.

"You hear anything?" asked Waldrip in a cautious whisper.

"Just the horses," said Harve.

"There's somebody down there, though," said Waldrip. "I'm bettin' them Injuns are after the horses. I'll go down and take a look."

"I don't believe they'd steal the horses," said Harve. "Go to sleep, Price. They'll be all right."

"No, I'm goin' for a looksee," insisted Waldrip.

There was a rustling sound as though he was coming out of his bedroll.

"Oh, shoot, if anybody's goin', it'll be me." Harve threw back his blankets and groped for his boots, found them and began pulling them on.

He couldn't let Price Waldrip do his job for him. He mentally swore at the chill that stiffened his boots, but finally tugged them on and stood up, stamping them into their accustomed shape.

Price Waldrip was already out there, a dark shape in the night with a pistol in his hand. "You stay with the horses," he ordered. "I'll see about it." Then he vanished from sight, soundless as the breeze that suddenly fanned Harve's cheek, coming down the draw. Automatically, he made a mental note that the wind had shifted. He moved slowly toward the horses, talking to them in a low voice so they wouldn't spook as he knew they would if he appeared suddenly.

A movement, a sound, a shadow warned him. He stopped, deadstill, with the impression someone was near. A little chill

21

ran up his spine and it wasn't all the night cold. He made small movements, easing his gun out of the holster, at the same going, moving slowly forward.

A gun spat in his face. He clubbed with the pistol instead of pulling the trigger, feeling the gun land on target.

He plunged ahead, grappling with the man, getting a rank body smell as they went to the ground, rolling over and over. The pistol was knocked out of his hand when Harve hit the ground, bouncing away. The man he wrestled with was powerful as a bull and seemed to be all fist, elbow and knee. The man knocked himself loose from Harve and scrambled away, his feet making a light patter through the brush while the horses snorted and danced in fright.

Trying to soothe the frightened animals Harve heard a hoarse shout from the direction of the crossing and a single pistol shot echoed through the draw.

On his feet, Harve plunged down the draw toward the crossing. He neared the ford and the sand muffled his footsteps. There were several riders out there, he could hear the hoof beats, a low sound of voices, and then he stumbled over a prostrate form stretched across his path.

He saved himself from falling heavily on the man by using his hands. There was a sudden flurry of hoof beats and then silence.

Harve listened for a moment before striking a match. Price Waldrip was lying in the sand with blood running from a gash along the side of his head, above his right ear. When Harve moved him into a more comfortable position, he groaned. Harve half-carried and half-dragged him up the draw to the camp and let him down on his bedroll.

There was a neat pile of wood Price had stacked for the morning fire and in a short time, Harve had a blaze that lighted the area. He turned to find Price staring at him.

"Sure walked into that one," he said wryly, "just like any rock-headed tenderfoot. But I just got grazed. Nothin' to worry about."

Harve didn't answer that but knelt beside Waldrip and looked carefully at the wound.

"Should have something on it. Turpentine, maybe. But I don't have any with me." He sounded discouraged.

Price Waldrip laughed. "Skip it, boy. It's already stopped bleeding. It'll scab over and when the scab's gone that'll be the end of it."

"All right, if you say so," Harve said doubtfully. He·looked at Waldrip. "Was it them Indians?"

"Don't think so," Waldrip said unhesitatingly.

Harve nodded agreement. "They made a noise down at the crossing. On purpose, I reckon. Anyway, they sent another man around to take the horses while we went down there to investigate. Except it didn't work out like they planned." He grinned at Price companionably. "I hit at that ranny with my pistol instead of shootin' him."

Price raised himself on one elbow. "I thought I heard a shot just before I got this one. He didn't hit you?"

Harve shook his head. "I was so close I could touch him. And I did with my pistol barrel. We wrestled around and then he took off. I lost my gun but come daylight I'll find it."

"We don't have to worry about 'em comin' back,' Waldrip said with conviction. "Let's get some shuteye, pardner."

Lying in his blankets, Harve had a warm feeling. A man like Price Waldrip had called him partner. They were partners. They'd went to war together. That made a difference, a big difference, no matter how small the war. *Too bad old Price wasn't going to hang around,* Harve thought. They'd make a team. He went to sleep thinking about that and his thoughts were good.

III

"Now SEE HERE, Harve," Price Waldrip said, when they got the smoke of Rowel over a ridge the next morning. "Ain't no use you payin' out good money to put these nags up while you talk business. I'll just hold 'em out on the edge of town while you chin with the banker."

"By golly, old man Racker'll be tickled pink to save a little money," Harve declared. He'd forgot all about the lecture Price had just finished, all about how you do a man a favor he'll pay you back by kicking your teeth out.

"Then it's a go," Waldrip said. "You ride on ahead, Harve. And when you've made your dicker, come back and we'll drive 'em in."

"Thanks a heap, Price," the kid said and passed the lead rope to Waldrip. He waved his hand and loped ahead while Price wrangled the remuda to keep them from following. Harve laughed out loud at the sight of the horses neighing and dancing, wanting to stay with him.

He still had that warm feeling for Price. *Stuck out on that damn ranch so long,* he thought, *I forgot how a human behaves. Can't figure old man Racker as human. He don't act it. That Waldrip's a mighty nice fellow. Wouldn't mind working with a man like that. Wonder if I could talk Racker into giving him a job?* Harve grinned wryly at the thought. In the first place, Racker wasn't taking on anyone else. And in the second place, a man like Price Waldrip wouldn't be interested in a forty a month riding job. Harve knew that without being told.

What, he wondered, *did Price do for a living?*

He didn't have time to think about that question because the town was coming up fast. He pulled the roan out of a lope on the edge of town and walked the horse over the plank bridge that spanned the trickle of brown water that was Rowel River. There, on the town side of the river, under a spread of silvery-leafed cottonwoods was Herman Bradley's blacksmith shop with a cluster of ponies at the hitch rail, waiting to be shod, and the cheerful noise of iron on iron rang in Harve's ears. The sun was warm and he could see the big leather-aproned giant of a man over the anvil, his arm raised rhythmically to deliver blows to the cherry-red iron. Harve's spirits lifted and he shifted in the saddle,

24

hungrily taking in the sights and sounds of a lively town.

The Butterfield Line corral loomed up and a fine-looking lot of horses they used, Harve thought, as he looked on the sleek animals munching hay out of a well-filled rack. Past that, and a row of buildings, and there was the Grand Central, an elegant hotel with gingerbread trim all around the upstairs balcony, curtains over the front windows, and down below, there was a gleam of brass through the swinging doors that led to the bar attached to the hotel.

Racker's voice came to him out of nowhere. *Stay out of the Central, Harve. Ain't no fit place for a kid.* Harve swore mildly. Beyond the hotel was the Wells Fargo, the bank, and farther on down a big rig pulled by six mules heaved and groaned into Potts' Wagon Yard, where the freighting rigs put in, and on down the line of business establishments; a bakery and a millinery shop and a leather shop, all flung together in one big building that went up three whole stories. Red brick, too. Harve leaned his head back and looked at the topmost story. *Mighty high building that,* he thought; *sure hate to fall off that roof.*

On the other side of the street was the mercantile store and Emily Clutt's laundry, a scattering of saloons and Frobacker's Pool Hall. *Harve,* Racker's voice came from nowhere again, *stay out of Frobacker's, Harve.*

Harve put the roan into the watering trough in front of the bank and let the horse fill up, while he savored the noise and excitement and smells of Rowel. A big, sandy-haired man came out of the Grand Central and sauntered toward the bank.

Marshal Bill Pelley, by crackie! Harve muttered to himself and felt his heart jump. It was said Bill Pelley killed a man most every night. *Don't look so doggone tough,* Harve thought, as he watched the big man from the corner of his eye. *Sort of meek, just like any old geezer.*

Pelley passed, nodding and giving Harve a twitch of his lips. "Howdy," he said.

Harvey returned the nod and said, "Fine, howdy."

25

He let the roan sniff at the water, watching Pelley walk on down the street, stopping to talk to this one and that. Harve felt his spirit soar like an eagle on an updraft. *Nothing like town,* he thought, *after a long, dry spell at Racker's, with the old man whining the whole long day about this, that and the other.*

When the roan raised its dripping muzzle and started looking around, just as fascinated as Harve, he got down and looped the reins through a ring bolt, hitched his pants up and bowlegged along the splintery plank walk toward the bank. He went inside, blinking in the gloom.

A thin-faced man at the teller's cage nodded without missing a beat counting the stack of gold pieces. He was as handy as a crap dealer Harve had seen once over at the Grand Central, peering through the window, of course. Harve walked up and stood by the wicket.

The thin-faced man finished counting and looked up with his eyebrows making a couple of dark v's on his high forehead. "What can I do for you, sonny?" he asked and then lowered his brows like he had a ready-made answer. "From Racker's, ain't you?"

Harve nodded, uncomfortable in his surroundings and trying to keep it a secret. "Mr. Racker sent me in."

The thin man pulled down the black sleeve protectors and pushed a green eyeshade up on his forehead. "Come along back, sonny," he said and turned and left the cage and went around and held the swinging gate open for Harve.

Harve went into the tiny enclosure and took the cane-bottom chair beside a roll-top desk. The thin man waited until Harve was seated and then lifting his coattails so he wouldn't sit on them, plumped down in a swivel chair. He looked at the kid and asked, "How's Racker?"

"Fair," said Harve, "when he ain't hurtin'."

Mr. Purvis, the banker, shook his head. "Don't see how he stands it," and with that, disposed of the human element. His voice became brisk and businesslike. "Let's get along with his business. I'm liable to get rushed just before noon."

"Mr. Racker wanted you to figure the note," Harve said. "Ain't got quite enough to make it, the way he figured it."

"Hum, hum," Mr. Purvis said severely and took a folder from his desk draw. "Not quite enough, huh?" He made it sound real bad.

Harve hastily explained. "I brought in some horses to sell to make up the difference," he said eagerly. "Good horses, easy sold."

Mr. Purvis' long face brightened. "Good, good," he said. He drew a fresh sheet of paper to him and began putting down figures. He muttered as he scribbled and Harve twisted in his chair and looked out through the doorway. Men and women out there coming and going, and all the loneliness of Racker's place seemed remote and far away. *Something doing around here,* Harve thought, *every minute of the day.*

Purvis clearing his throat brought Harve back into the room. "Comes to $487.52," said Purvis. "How much you shy?"

"Eighty-seven fifty-two," Harve said and stood up and began unloosening the money belt.

"Hold it," said Purvis, pushing his palms toward Harve. "Just keep it all until you get all of it. Easier to keep track of that way."

Harve tucked his shirttail back into his pants. "Yes, sir," he said.

"Where you holdin' them horses?" asked Purvis.

"I met a fellow," Harve said. "He's keepin' them out on the edge of town. Save a lot on the bill that way."

Purvis' face lengthened. "Know him?"

"Just met him," Harve said. "We met on the road, over by Pipestem Springs."

"Good Lord," Purvis groaned. "He won't be there, boy, when you get back. You been took."

Harve drew in a deep breath. "You—you think he stole 'em?"

"I'm pretty darn sure of it," Purvis said in a manner that

left no room for argument. "He just took you in, boy. That was a fool thing to do."

"Maybe—maybe he'll be there," Harve said faintly.

Purvis shook his head. "You'll see. What're you going to do now, boy?"

"I'll ride out and see," Harve cried, his heart a leaden weight inside him. Old Price wouldn't do that to him. Or would he? He went through the swinging gate and trotted out the door. His fingers shook as he untied his horse. He swung up on the pony and the startled horse jumped from seldom-used spurs.

IV

HARVEY THUNDERED over the plank bridge and his heart did a flip when he saw the blank expanse of mesa stretching away to the mountains. Not a living thing moved in that wide expanse of gray sage. He rode on at an easy canter and then pulled the roan to a sliding halt at the sound of a voice.

Price Waldrip called again and Harve swiveled his head. The big dark man sat in the grass beside the river and the horse herd grazed in a nearby draw. Price grinned his wide white grin at Harvey and called, "What's the big hurry, Harve?"

Harve put the roan over that way and dismounted, keeping his back to Price so Waldrip wouldn't see the relief on his face. He fumbled at his cinch for a moment and then turned. "Reckon I was in a hurry," he said. "Thought you'd be holdin' 'em further out a piece."

Still grinning, Waldrip got up and dusted the seat of his pants. "They grazed over this way and I just followed," he said. "Make a deal?"

Harve shook his head. "No, just checked with the bank. So as to see how much I was shy."

"Well, let's move 'em on in," Price said, stepping up into his saddle. "I'm getting a mite thirsty. And hungry, too."

Harve discarded the impulsive notion to tell Waldrip how scared he'd been, and why. "Me too," he said and got on the roan and rode over and got the lead rope and pulled the string away from the rich grass. He was hungry, he suddenly realized. He felt his spirits lift and he chuckled inwardly, remembering how downright scared he'd been, thinking Price Waldrip had made off with Racker's horses. A thin stream of guilt spread through him as he watched the broad back ahead, thinking how he'd judged Price guilty so quick. *That was Purvis,* he thought defensively. *Suspicious lot, them bankers.*

Price let his tall black drift back beside Harvey. "Fella came by while you was gone," he said. "Acted like he might be interested in buyin' your horses, Harve."

"That's the reason I'm here," Harve said. "He say where we can find him?"

Waldrip nodded. "He's in the business. Name of Buckner."

"I know him," Harve said. "A sharp jasper on a horse deal."

Waldrip grinned. "Thing is to be sharper," he said. "How much did you figure to get, Harve?"

Harve looked at the sky and then leaned forward to spat. "Maybe twenty-five a head."

"He'll go that," Waldrip said positively. "Maybe higher. Start it off by asking thirty-five, Harve."

Harve whistled. "Zingies! They'd never bring thirty-five, Price," he protested. "I was goin' to ask twenty-five and take as low as fifteen."

Waldrip kept grinning good-naturedly. "Don't never try givin' anything away," he said, looking at Harve, his grin fading. "You do what I say, boy and you won't go wrong. Start at thirty-five. I'll back you up."

"Stand at my back until my belly gets beat blue?" Harve asked with chuckle.

"I'm not kiddin', Harve," Price said quietly.

Sudden decision flooded Harvey. "Sure thing, Price," he said. "I was just funnin'."

"Thatsa kid," Price said.

They walked the horses through town, leading the string into the traders beyond the wagon yard. A tall, loose-jointed man came out of a tiny shack with a gleam of recognition in his eyes.

"Howdy, Waldrip," Sam Buckner, the horse trader drawled. "You come along mighty quick."

"Harve here, got back quicker'n I thought he would," Waldrip said easily. "He's the ramrod on this deal, Sam. You'll have to dicker with him."

Buckner's small gray eyes flicked to Harvey. "How's Racker?" he asked and his eyes sharpened as he looked at the horses bunched together. He walked around them and then went close to examine the foreleg of a gray that had been wirecut.

"Why Racker's all right," Harve said at Waldrip's frown and nod. "Except when the pain hits him. . . . That gray got wirecut this spring. Healing good, another month you'll never know he had it."

"Seein' as how it's a crippled man's horses," Buckner said with a judicious squint, "I reckon I might go a little over their worth. Say twenty dollars a head."

Waldrip reached for the lead rope and jerked the horse's head toward the street.

Buckner's mouth opened and he stared and then said, "Hey, what's the big idea?"

"You don't want to do business with us," Waldrip said, smoothly, "Does he, Harve?"

Harve stared, open-mouthed as Buckner, unable to speak.

"Don't be too all-fired hurrified," Buckner said testily. "I had to start som'ers, didn't I?" He opened the gray's mouth and leaned down to look at the long yellow teeth of the horse. "Might be we could do a mite better." He stepped to another horse and examined another set of teeth.

Under Waldrip's prodding eyes, Harve made himself speak. "How'd it do to start at thirty-five?" he asked. His voice sounded thin and piping to him. His fingers sought the tobacco sack in his shirt pocket.

"Thirty-five?" Buckner snorted. "You been out there too long, sonny, all by yourself."

Harve turned red, felt his face burn and his fingers shook the tobacco out of the paper. He crumpled it up and let the wind take it away.

"Harve broke them all himself," Waldrip said with a smoothness Harvey envied. "First class job, too. Not a bad actor in the bunch. Harve knows his horses."

Buckner frowned. "How about thirty?" he asked, shaking his head at his own stupidity. "That's more'n they're worth but Racker bein' crippled an' all—"

Harve opened his mouth to accept and then closed it when Price shook his head in a warning negation.

"You're not buyin' a pig in a poke," Waldrip said, with honey dripping from his words. "All sound as a dollar, Sam, and Racker will stand back of 'em, won't he, Harve?"

Harve nodded dumbly, enthralled with Waldrip's argument. *Hope some of that rubs off on me,* he thought.

"I know what they're worth," Buckner said, a stubborn tilt to his head. He spread his legs and jammed his hands in his pockets.

Waldrip winked at Harve. "Done," he said, easy and grinning a look-here wide stretching of his lips at Harve. "All but here's something to think about—Racker'll be here tomorrow and a year from tomorrow to back 'em up. Good horses are hard to come by and nobody knows that better than you. Everybody in the country's heard of Sam Buckner."

"Yeah," Buckner said.

"Sure. You hold 'em long enough, feed 'em good, brush 'em down, you'll get fifty, seventy-five easy enough."

Buckner swore conversationally, calling on God to witness his honesty and integrity. "Thirty-two fifty is the best I can do."

Waldrip winked at Harve. "Done," he said, easy and grinn-

31

ing a look-here wide stretching of his lips at Harve. "All right, Harve?"

Harve said, "Gosh, yes."

"Come on then," Buckner said gruffly, "and get your money."

While Buckner counted out the money, Harve asked him, "You know Price Waldrip long?"

Buckner stopped counting and looked up at Harve, squinting. "Met him this mornin'," he said shortly. "Thought maybe he was workin' for Racker, too."

"No," said Harve. "I just met him."

Buckner stopped counting again, looking at the money on the table and the money in his hand. Then without looking at Harvey, he said, "I was you, I'd watch that jasper, Harvey."

The money, more than three hundred dollars in gold, was heavy in Harve's pockets as he and Waldrip walked their horses down the street to the Grand Central.

"I'm gonna hotfoot it right to the bank," Harve said, "and get Racker's business done with."

"Time enough." Waldrip grinned. "We deserve a drink on that deal, Harve." He tied his black to the hitchrack, winking at Harve in a manner that admitted him to the club of happy saddlemates.

Harve, feeling reluctant, looped his reins over the rail and followed the big man across the plank walk. "Reckon we can do that," he said, thinking at the same time that he should be taking care of Racker's business, first thing. Racker was always telling him: "First things first, boy, business before pleasure," and all kind of stuff like that. A stubborn resistance to Racker's best interest rose in him. *Heck with it,* he thought. Too, he didn't want Waldrip to think he wasn't dry behind the ears yet; anyway, there was time for Racker's business later.

And knowing Racker, he realized the crusty old devil wouldn't be any more grateful if he learned Price Waldrip had got a better price for the horses than he could have done, working it all by his lonesome. Always complaining, no matter what; that was Racker's way. Harvey suddenly dreaded the thought of going back to the ranch and putting up with Racker's daylong whining. "Yeah, man, let's go see the elephant," he said.

Price's heavy hand fell on his shaking him lightly. "That's the stuff," he said, "an' we'll listen to them owls. After pulling a deal like we did with Buckner we got it comin'."

Harve followed Price into the Grand Central. The glitter of that bar made him blink. The atmosphere of the Grand Central was loud and cheerful. Two busy bartenders dispensed drinks to a thirsty crowd. The clink of chips and the whir of roulette wheels overrode the hum of voices and the soft but penetrating calls of the croupier, chuck-a-luck and and faro dealers. "Come on, boy, don't stand there with your eyes buggin' out," Waldrip said, and pulled Harve after him.

Waldrip stopped at the free lunch and put together a mass of rye bread, cheese, roast beef, mustard, ketchup and pickles, urging Harvey to follow his example because his mouth was full. Harvey made a sandwich exactly like Waldrip's, and followed his new friend to a table.

"Straight shot with a beer on the side," Waldrip told the bartender and Harve nodded agreement. *This is all right,* he thought with satisfaction, putting down the inward unrest at not finishing Racker's errand.

The bartender brought the drinks and Waldrip plunked down a gold coin in a careless manner. His bright black eyes were on Harve as he raised the shot glass to his full lips. Harve noted Waldrip's lips, very red, making him seem healthy and full of vitality.

"Here's how, pardner," Waldrip said and tossed the drink down, neat.

Harve aped his motions. The hot liquor burned his throat and he felt its warm passage down his throat and into his stomach, where it seemed to spread a warm glow all through him. He coughed and his eyes watered. "Man alive!" he gasped, and sipped the beer.

Price Waldrip grinned at him and bit into the sandwich he held in his two hands and worked his jaws. "You really put it over on Buckner, Harve," he said as he chewed. "Good trader, boy, that's what you are."

Harve's shirt felt tight from his swelling chest. He didn't even mind Waldrip calling him "boy." The way Waldrip said it wasn't at all like the banker calling him "sonny" the way he had. Harve figure he was pretty lucky running into a man like Waldrip. The world seemed full of doggone nice people Harve reflected, as he ate. "Wasn't nothin' much," he mumbled.

Suddenly, the food was gone, and the drinks, too. Harve belched. "Guess I better take care of my horse," he said, rising, "an' the other stuff."

"Take my black to the livery, too," Waldrip said. "And hurry back, Harve. We ain't seen that elephant yet."

"Well, maybe I better—".

"Be sure he gets some grain." Waldrip grinned and waved Harve on his way.

Coming back from the livery, Harve was surprised when Marshal Bill Pelley met him and stopped. "Who's the big fellow who rode in with you, sonny?" the lawman asked.

"Hey, he's sure big," said Harve. "Big enough to go bear huntin' with a switch. He's—"

"Sonny, I asked you a question," Pelley said in a soft but steely voice.

Harve felt his cheeks burn. There was that "sonny" stuff again. Dammit, didn't folks realize he was near old enough to vote. Well, maybe not, three years being such a long time. Only time anyone called him a man was when there was a man's work to be done.

"Fella named Waldrip," Harve said. "Price Waldrip's his full tag."

Pelley nodded thoughtfully. "Known him long?"

34

"Why, sure," Harve said carelessly. "Old buddy from way back, Marshal."

Pelley lowered his head, looking at Harve from under his hat brim and wrinkling his forehead. "You sure, sonny?"

"Durn right I'm sure," Harve said shortly and pushed on by the marshal, thinking, *dang-take it, yesterday I'd've give my right arm to talk to Bill Pelley and here today I'm being snappish with him. Must be that drink or two I had.* He couldn't hardly remember how many drinks he'd had before taking the horses to the livery.

Back in the Grand Central, there were two ladies with Price Waldrip. Harve stood back, feeling nervous and undecided, until Price spotted him. The big man jumped up and motioned at Harve and then came slowly to meet him.

"Hey, pardner, we got some company since you been gone," he said. "Lookie, this is Belle"—he gestured to a dark-eyed woman with a surprisingly serene face, a woman who smiled at Harve—"and this here is mine, Tiny, and don't you go makin' no eyes at her." Tiny was a tall, buxom girl with long, golden hair. She giggled at Harve, as Price pushed him into a seat next to Belle.

Belle immediately sat on Harve's lap to Price Waldrip's uproarious laughter. Harve felt his face burning. He could feel the tight clothing that pressed against Belle's flesh, could feel the ribs of a corset and smelled the rich odor of perfume in his nostrils and felt the tendrils of hair tickling his face. She was saying something but he couldn't hear.

"What's that?" Harve asked.

"I just asked your name, honey," Belle said.

"Why, it's Harve," Harvey said, "Harvey Holley." He could see wrinkles around her eyes and on her neck now that he was close to her. He no longer felt the weight of her on his thighs and she stood there looking down at him.

"Holley?" she breathed. "You Hack Holley's boy?" Without waiting for Harve to answer she wheeled and bent forward, searching Price Waldrip's laughing face. "He is, he is. You come with me, Price! We have some talk to make."

She went away at a swift walk without waiting to see if Price Waldrip was following.

Price got up slowly, not smiling. He looked at Tiny and then at Harve. "You get lost, Tiny, I'll see you later. Me and Harve got to twist the tiger's tail when I get back."

He followed Belle up the stairs.

Harve gulped. "Is—is he goin' up to her room?" he asked in a scandalized voice.

Tiny didn't seem to notice his agitation. She adjusted her hat with a big purple plume and glanced at him. "That he is, sonny," she said, rising to her full height, nearly six feet, Harve judged. "But he won't be long, I promise you."

Harve watched her saunter to the bar and almost immediately a cowboy bought her a drink. Harve watched the stairs anxiously.

Once away from the lower floor of the Grand Central, Price Waldrip made no pretense of affability. His fingers closed around Belle's arm and tightened until she made a sound of pain. He shoved her through the door which she had just unlocked and went in, closing it after him.

"What're you tryin' to do, mess things up?" he asked coldly.

Her eyes were dry now, with only a trace of the tears she'd shed coming up the stairs, but her face was pale. She looked at him steadily for a long, stretching moment while a piano began tinkling down below and a wave of sudden merriment washed over them.

"You didn't tell me he'd be here. You didn't tell me anything. What is it you're trying to do, Price?"

A wolfish grin appeared on his handsome face and was gone so quickly it might have never been there. His black eyes held steady on her. "I was about his age when Hack took me on," he said. "Just as raw and wet behind the ears as he is. Hack was a mighty big man to me. I thought he made the thunder and lightnin'." He grinned at her. "I guess you know all about that."

36

She flushed redly. "What's that got to do with here and now?" She turned suddenly, not able to withstand the sear of his eyes any longer. "Hack's gone. There's nothing left of him but that boy down there. And a bad name. What're you trying to do with that boy, Price?" She was unable to keep the anguish out of her voice.

"Like I said I was about Harve's age," Price said, not a trace of anger in his voice but a coldness that sent a chill around the woman's heart. "I looked up to him and he taught me a lot. He got himself killed and I went to jail. I need that money he left with Burt Racker to take care of the kid. I mean to get it one way or another."

"That was a long time ago," she said tonelessly. "Maybe the money's gone. Anyway, what do you want me to do?"

"I may need you," he said. "Come on back down stairs and don't let on. Not about nothin'."

She slowly turned with a resolve that hardened her face, showing her age. "I won't do it," she said in a hard flat voice. "I won't leave this room as long as he's in town. I'd rather die!"

He laughed, a hard, merciless sound that isolated them in the room. "Maybe you won't need to, but if I think you have to, you will. You will, Belle, or you'll wish to hell you had."

"Leave that boy alone."

He laughed again and she shivered. "Hell, you sound like a mother, Belle." He turned and walked out the door. As he pulled it shut he had a glimpse of her, with shoulders drooped, head down. He chuckled softly as he walked down the dim hallway, toward the noisy saloon below.

Harvey Holley breathed a sigh of relief when he caught sight of Price Waldrip's tall form on the stairs. The big man pushed his way to the table and dropped into the chair he'd had before he left, signaling the bartender with two fingers. "You ain't been drinkin'," he told Harve in an accusing voice.

"Waiting for you, Price," Harve said nonchalantly. "Didn't want to get way out in front all by my lonesome."

The bartender brought the drinks and Price paid for them. There were more drinks and then more and still Harvey hadn't been able to pay for a round.

"Keep your money," Price said with a crooked grin. "You come by yours a lot harder than I do."

Price seemed to have plenty of money, Harve thought hazily. He readily agreed to go to the dice table, and he remembered walking tall toward the green covered table, taking high knee-lifting steps that seemed to float him there.

Price Waldrip grinned at Harve while he rolled the dice. He seemed to have an endless supply of money. He lost a good two months wages by Harvey's estimate and there still seemed to be plenty left. Then it was dark, the bank was closed and the world turned into a misty blur that was bright lights, music, gusts of laughter, and voices which gradually receded into nothing. . . .

V

HARVE AWOKE SLOWLY, his mind flinching from reality, from guilt, even before he came fully to life.

When a man pulls a shenanigan, he thought, *lying down on the job and not doing what has to be done, he feels like not waking up at all.* But Price Waldrip was whistling cheerfully and washing noisily in the big thick white wash bowl, splashing water on his face and bubbling into his two cupped hands like a thirsty mule. Harve rolled up on one elbow, his insides leaden and remorse bearing down on him.

The big dark man saw Harve's reflection in the mirror. He turned, his head tilted, swabbing at his ears with the towel, grinning like a treed coon.

"How you feel, bronc twister?" he asked cheerfully and tossed the towel to the rack.

38

Harve tried a grin and his face felt like it cracked. "All right, I reckon," he said without conviction and swung his feet to the floor. The room spun dizzily and he lay down quickly before he fell. He lay there with his eyes squeezed shut. Then he opened them cautiously and gingerly raised himself again. The world was a steadier place and he slowly got to his feet. His clothing was scattered around the room helter-skelter. The money belt, so carefully guarded, drooped across a chair back. He stumbled to it and lifted it. There was no cheerful clink of gold coin inside it. He turned toward Waldrip, the sick feeling worsening.

"Where—where's the money?"

Waldrip kept grinning. "You was bettin' the field, Harve. Don't you remember nothin'?"

Harve shook his head, feeling the strong leaden thump of his heart pumping blood to his aching head, causing it to throb even more. "Did—did I gamble?"

"Did you gamble?" Waldrip threw back his head and opened his mouth, braying like a hound. "Man alive, you was hot as grandma's house the day it burnt down. Seventeen passes and you let it all ride. Then you put everything on the next roll!"

Harve tried to swallow the swelling in his throat, his sense of foreboding increasing to unbearable proportions. "Wha—what happened then?"

Waldrip scrubbed his right boot against the calf of his leg. "You threw snake eyes," he said casually and slipped on his coat. "Come on Harve boy, get dressed. I'm hungrier than a hydrophobia skunk."

"Yeah," Harve muttered and dressed listlessly, while Waldrip watched him from a seat on the bed, whistling tunelessly. He was aware of Waldrip's speculative gaze as he splashed cold water on his face and head, dried and combed his tangled yellow hair. "What'm I gonna do?" he asked unhappily. *Dad burn it, anyway, how could I do a thing like that? What would old man Racker say now?* He damned himself for being seventeen different kinds of fool.

Waldrip rose from his seat on the bed, laughing, and came over to clap a heavy hand on Harve's shoulder. "Do? Hell's fire, man, don't worry about it. I think mebbe I can he'p you out."

Harve's face brightened and his head lifted hopefully, his shoulders losing the shape of defeat. "How, Price, how?"

Waldrip kept grinning. "Like I said, don't worry none. The time comes and we'll square everything up. We can't make medicine on an empty belly, boy. Come on!" With a careless wave of his hand he swung toward the door.

Harve followed, wanting to ask questions, not able to think of any of them. He trailed after Price, down the stairs and up the street to Homer's Chuckwagon, right next door to McGuffey's General Store. He shoved his hat on the back of his head, determined to have his say and get it off his chest.

He didn't have a chance because Price started banging on the counter with both hands. "Gotta get some fodder under my belt," he declared. "What're you gonna have, Harve?"

Harve sat there, feeling confused, conscious that all eating had suspended for the moment, while early patrons regarded Price with amusement, tolerance, and some, especially Marshal Bill Pelley, with disapproval.

"I'll take what they got," Harve said.

Price opined he'd take a little bit of everything and Homer shuffled off to the kitchen.

Well, by grab, Harve thought, *if he don't want to listen on an empty belly he don't have to.* The main thing, Price had a solution to his problem. He felt better, shoving back his sleeves as Homer came bearing ham and eggs and pancakes, with his little finger hooked in a jug of sorghum syrup. That hope held out by Price gave Harve an appetite for the food.

Harve carried that hope with him all through his enormous breakfast and the many cups of scalding coffee. Afterward, with a cigarette between his lips, he felt like the reasonable picture of a human being once more.

"Now, Price," he said, "how do I do it?"

Waldrip carefully wiped his lips with the back of his hand and using his thumb and forefinger stroked his mustaches into spikes. "Come along," he said, rising.

They strolled out on the plank walk. Price turned toward the hotel corral, back of the Grand Central. There, near the barn, he stopped looking at the horses beyond the pole bars of the corral. He negligently leaned against the peeled logs and turned, gesturing toward the street. Through the alley, Harve saw the stage swing into the space before the hotel. The hind wheels of the stage showed beyond the building. Waldrip looked at Harve with narrowed eyes. "It's easy, Harve," he said. "Let's walk down there and look at the stage unload."

They emerged from the alley and took seats on the bench outside the hotel entrance and watched the passengers emerge stiffly from the dusty vehicle and walk uncertainly into the hotel. A Wells Fargo clerk came from the office near the hotel and walked over to the stage and took the strongbox which the shotgun guard handed down.

"See that box, Harve?" Waldrip asked in a low, tight voice. "The one ol' Well Fargo's man is takin in?"

Harve nodded dumbly, the pulse in his temples pounding an ache back into his skull.

"Empty now" Waldrip said. "But when the stage goes north, it's loaded. Plumb to th' brisket. All we do is take it."

Harve's voice was a croak. "A—a holdup?"

Waldrip laughed but it didn't sound much like a laugh to Harve. "Yeah. It's easy as fallin' off a hoss, Harve."

Harve rose and moved away in one swift, fluid motion. "Not me," he said in a hoarse voice. "Not me." He went down the walk.

Waldrip's rough hand fell on his shoulder. "Don't be a consarn dang fool," he said easily, laughing softly. "Them

41

as has, takes. And you ain't got no choice, Harve. You'll go to jail for certain you don't pay Racker's note and take back the change. This way, you'll get what you need and enough left over to tell Racker where to go."

"He's been fair with me," Harve said miserably.

"Like fun he has," Waldrip declared. "I listened to you, Harve. I know what you've had to put up with from that old turkey buzzard. I'm showin' you a way out."

Harve jerked away from Waldrip's restraining hand. "I don't want to listen," he said, in that same hoarse scared voice. "Leave me out of it, Price."

Waldrip watched him walk away and he laughed again. "I'll be up in the room, Harve," he called.

Harve plunged heedlessly away. All he wanted to do was get away from the convincing persuasion of Price Waldrip. *Golly gee,* he thought, *maybe Price is a regular holdup man. He is sure loaded with money and he spends it like it was going outta style. He's a good hombre to steer clear of and that's what I'm gonna do.*

He glanced up and saw the skinny banker, Mr. Purvis, bearing down on him like a hungry chicken after a june bug. Harve stopped short and looked wildly around. Mr. Purvis wanted that money and he didn't have it. Harve turned and bolted down the nearby alley, ignoring Mr. Purvis' hail. He ran through the alley, his heart pounding, feeling guilty as sin itself.

Emerging from the alley, Harve dogtrotted to the Grand Central stable. He went back in the dim interior, smelling the familiar odors of nitrogen, hay and leather and gathering some small measure of comfort from the familiarity. He walked on back until he found his horse. He stood by the roan, pondering his future, which seemed very bleak at the moment.

He had to pay Racker's note. That was important because otherwise the old man would lose his ranch. He didn't want that to happen. If only he had taken care of Racker's business in the first place he wouldn't be up to his eyeballs in the pickle barrel now.

"Oh, boy! Come outta there, boy!"

He shivered at the sound of Mr. Purvis shouting from the front entrance to the barn. How in tarnation did he know where to look? Like a cornered rabbit, Harve ran up and down the stall, disturbing the roan which snorted and stamped. He glanced wildly around. There was a small window in the stall, opening into the corral. He went past his horse, patting the sleek neck and hoisted himself up to the sill and squeezed through. He dropped to the ground and went along the weathered board wall to the rear. He was filled with a sense of shame as he crawled through the peeled poles and walked stiff-legged past a big manure pile and on down the back of the stores fronting the main street. When he came to the alley by the wagon yard he cut through to the main street and walked rapidly toward the hotel.

He hesitated at the hotel entrance. Price was up there waiting for him with an out for him.

He hesitated again and then hearing Purvis' strident command to come out of the barn, he turned into the hotel.

VI

MARSHAL WILLIAM TECUMSEH PELLEY, since his employment as sole arbiter of law and order in Rowel, adopted one unvarying policy. He never did anything on routine. He varied his hours but was never far away for any pressing emergency. He might appear in the Grand Central or any of the other saloons for that matter, at any hour of the day and night. Sometimes he had breakfast at the Chuckwagon but you couldn't bet on seeing him there. He purposely changed his day to day routine so that vengeance-seeking bushwhackers could not plan ahead.

He enforced the relatively simple laws with a singlemindedness that some people considered highhanded, swearing that when election time came around they'd vote out of office the city fathers who brought Pelley in.

He had his supporters, good men and bad.

Pelley arrived in Rowel with a reputation ready-made in Tombstone, a taciturn man, softspoken, slow-talking and as quick to act as a striking rattler. Troublemakers walked softly around Bill Pelley. He was not a man to trifle with. He stood six-one without his high-heel boots, took meticulous care of his health and clothing and watched his town with the eye of an eagle. A brown-faced man, his cool gray eyes missed nothing that went on in Rowel, the conglomeration of frame, log and brick that to a strange eye seemed flung down by a careless giant in a moment of childish rage.

After breakfast at Homer's Chuckwagon, where he observed Price Waldrip and Harvey Holley with some disapproval, he smoked a cigar and then sauntered across the street to the hole-in-the-wall office provided him by the town council.

The new woman, Belle, was seated in the straight chair next to his desk. She rose as he entered and he removed his hat and took the cigar from his mouth.

"Ma'am," he said gravely.

"Marshal, I'm Belle Smith and I want to ask you a favor."

"Why, set down, Miss Belle and tell me all about it," he said, and with surprising courtliness held the chair for her.

When she was again seated, he dropped his hat to the floor beside his chair and sat down, observing her covertly as he ground out his cigar in a tin can he used for an ashtray.

"You don't have to put that out on account of me," she said.

"I had all I wanted," he answered, leaning back in his chair, studying her face carefully. "How can I help you, ma'am?"

"That boy, Harvey. You've seen him around?"

"He was whooping it up last night," Pelley said, his face impassive. "What about him?"

44

"I hardly know how to say it," she confessed.

"Just say what's on your mind," he said gently.

She smiled at him and thanked him with her eyes. "I—I'd simply like to ask you to tell him to get of of town. Get out before he gets in trouble."

Bill Pelley chuckled lightly. "It's a free country," he said. "The boy hasn't broke any law that I know about." He took another cigar from his pocket and smelled it, then replaced it. "I can't go around telling people to get out of town for no reason at all." He leaned forward, crossing his hands on the desk. "You care to tell me what this is all about?"

"He's so young. He's in bad company and he'll get in trouble. Can't you stop that before it happens?"

"Don't play poker, Miss Belle. You'd never be able to run a bluff and sometimes you have to do that." He opened a drawer in the desk and took out a handful of wanted posters and began going through them carefully. "I looked these over last night, looking for that 'bad company.' I didn't find a thing." He stopped shuffling the posters and eyed her steadily. "You know something about him I don't know?"

She shook her head. "I don't know him," she said in a small voice.

"You're a durn poor liar," he observed.

She started, flushing. "I want to get that boy out of this town," she said in a low voice.

"I'd kind of like that myself," he said. "Right now there ain't much I can do. But if it's any comfort, Purvis the banker is on the boy's trail. Purvis might put on enough pressure to get him back to the home place."

"Or somewhere," she said in a tight voice.

"Miss Belle, you're working yourself up to a boil," Bill Pelley said gently, smiling. "You shouldn't ought to worry about a strange young fella who means nothing at all to you."

"That's one of the things wrong with this world," she said, "not enough people care about people." She rose and stood there staring down at him. "If you can't make him leave town, please watch him and see he doesn't get in trouble."

He had stood quickly when she rose to her feet. He said, "Don't you worry none, Miss Belle. I'll keep a lookout. It's a promise."

"Thank you, Marshal. I'll be going now." She turned then and hurried across the room and out the door. Pelley watched her for a moment. When he turned back to his desk he opened the drawer and dropped the wanted posters inside and closed it with a bang. The softness that was in him while he talked to the woman was gone.

He spent the day, idling around town, waiting for Harve to return. He knew that the boy had rented two horses, rode away, leading them. Harve had told the stableman he had to do some packing. Pelley speculated on these actions and though he had his ready-made answers he couldn't be certain. He walked Rowel's main street and as usual kept his eyes open. In late afternoon he saw Purvis enter the Grand Central Bar. When Purvis saw him, he came to stand beside him.

"Have a drink with me, Marshal," Purvis said.

"Don't care if I do. Thanks."

Purvis signaled the bartender, who brought a bottle and two glasses, which he placed on the polished surface. Purvis waited until the man moved away before he spoke. As he poured he said quietly, "That kid's been ducking me all day."

"He lost his roll," Pelley said. "He's wonderin' what he's gonna do about it."

"If I was the law I'd be wondering, too," Purvis said pointedly.

"What's that supposed to mean?"

"I don't know a thing about the big fellow," Purvis said. "But from all outward appearances I'd guess that he's made a few collections at gunpoint. He has the marks of an outlaw, Bill."

Pelley laughed. "You figure it that way, Mr. Purvis?"

46

The banker nodded. "He's up to something. And I believe he's using the boy for some dark purpose."

"Could be, could be," Pelley admitted. He raised his glass to Purvis and drank his whiskey neat. "I'm keeping an eye out if that's any satisfaction."

Purvis nodded. "Suits me fine, he said. "I hate to see that fine young man get into trouble he couldn't handle."

The silence between them grew. Purvis twiddled a glass between his fingers, casting sidelong glances at Pelley. Finally, he said, "There is another way, Marshal."

"Spill it, then."

"You could run that big fellow clean out of the country."

"I could do that," Pelley said, "but I won't."

Purvis looked surprised. "I know you're not scared of him," he said.

Pelley didn't answer that. "Kids have run into all kinds of problems," he said. "You can't keep 'em on a bottle forever. Take Harvey . . . he's a good boy and he'll make a fine man if he gets the chance. But how's he gonna develop if somebody rides herd on him from here on out?"

"I hadn't thought of that part of it," Purvis said. He started to fill Pelley's glass but the marshal stopped him with a wave of his hand.

A man ran into the saloon calling, "Marshal Pelley!" He saw Pelley and ran up to him, pointing breathlessly toward the door. "That Chinaman what works for Emily Clutt! He hit old Tobe with a hatchet and took off on Clancy's horse!"

"How's Tobe?" Pelley asked, striding away from the bar. The man followed close on his heels.

"Done for, I reckon."

"Saddle my horse," Pelley said, "while I get my rifle and a box of shells."

He walked to his office and took a Winchester from the gun rack and dumped a box of shells in his coat pocket. He went out and his horse was waiting. He mounted and rode off in the direction the Chinaman had fled.

He felt reluctant to go but he had to do it. He'd planned to watch for Harve and see what he was about. He had not seen Price Waldrip leave town soon after Harve departed. If he had he'd have been a lot more worried.

In a grove back of the blacksmith shop, Price Waldrip came on the three men who waited for him.

The man wearing two guns swaggered over to meet him. "Hi ya, Price," he said and waved at the two watching. "This here is Dingus and Squint."

"You just brought two?" Price asked unnecessarily. "You think that's enough, Wes?" He looked keenly at the two, seeing the usual type of follower that an outlaw like Wes Carney picked up. "Howdy, boys."

Dingus and Squint murmured, "Howdy."

"Don't sound like it's gonna be much of a job," Carney said.

"It won't. You three'll be enough." He squatted down and picked up a stick and smoothed out the dirt between his boots. "Now here—" He stopped speaking and looked up at Dingus and Squint. "You boys go on down to the Grand Central barn and saddle my black. His stall's third from the end on the right, a hell of a big black."

The two men looked at Carney who nodded. They tied Carney's horse to a tree and mounted their own animals. "Where's yore saddle?" Dingus, who appeared to be the smartest one of the two, asked.

"Right there alongside the horse," Price said "on the partition. Be sure that blanket is all smoothed out."

"I know how to saddle a hoss," Dingus said with dignity.

The two of them rode off, twisting in the saddle and looking back now and then.

Price drew the road up the valley toward Jemez Springs. "Here's where we'll stake out the horses," he told Carney. "You and your boys be waitin' at the top of the draw, after we get the box. After you take it from us, we'll head right

48

for Racker's place. Harve'll do whatever has to be done after we pull the stickup and then lose it."

Carney rubbed a palm over his mouth. "Seems like you're goin to an awful lot o' trouble," he said doubtfully.

Waldrip laughed. "Yeah. Well, it's worth it. Alongside what we can get from old Racker, that strongbox of Wells Fargo is peanuts."

"I don't figger how all this rigmarole works," Carney said.

Price rose and flung the stick from him. "Hell, it's plumb simple. Harve figgers he had everything corraled when we ride off with that money from the stage. Then you take it away from us. All the things that seemed to be all right suddenly ain't all right. We'll have to think up somethin' else then, and Racker's it!"

"Suppose he starts shootin' when we throw down on you?"

Waldrip chuckled softly. "He always looks at me 'fore he does anything, Wes. You got nothin' to worry about along that line. You can take my word for it."

"Well, all right. We'll get out soon as the boys get back."

"Here they come now," Waldrip said, and went to meet the two men leading his black.

He took the reins and stepped into the saddle, reining back toward town.

"I thought you was goin' the other way," Carney said.

Price grinned. "Yeah, but I got t' get that damn marshal out o' town first."

"How you gonna do that?" Carney said.

"I got it all figgered," Price said smoothly and touched spurs to his black.

Carney untied his horse and mounted. He sat there looking after Waldrip. "There goes one o' the smartest jaspers in the business," he said.

Dingus and Squint looked after Waldrip and said nothing.

"Well, come on," Carney said. "We'll camp in them little draws down by the river 'til mornin'."

49

"Why don't we stay in town?" Squint asked in a whiny voice.

"Because there'll be hell to pay in town real soon," Carney said. "Come on, let's ride."

VII

ONCE OUT OF ROWEL, leading the two horses, Harve let his roan pick its own way while he caught up on some thinking. He was excited as a range colt feeling the first rope. For all that, he knew if he didn't get some thinking behind him he'd never get it done; not after Price Waldrip overtook him. The big man kept him off balance and he couldn't think at all, let alone think straight.

He looked with a horseman's eye at the two horses he led. Not that he had to worry about them. Price told him any old kind of plugs would do. One of them kept lagging back, the lead rope taut. *Don't want to leave his barn,* Harve thought, *just like a lot of people.*

Crossing the bridge, the hoofs made their own thunder. On the far side from town, he left the road, urging the roan down along the edge of the willows and a few big cottonwoods that lined the bank. He kept on until a big growth of hackberry bushes came off up a shallow swale. He guided the roan in behind this screen and dismounted. He led the two haltered animals a little distance and tied them. Returning to the roan he loosened the cinches and let the animal graze, while he threw himself on the ground, picked up a long-stemmed straw and put it in his mouth. He listened to the wind and the brush talk back and forth; off beyond the leafy screen, a blue jay scolded some intruder.

Gotta do my thinking in a hurry because Price'll be along any minute now and then it'll be too late. But all the clear, cold analysis he'd planned didn't come off. He found he couldn't lay out the ifs, ands and whys so he could pick the best and let the rest go to grass. The sheer excitement of this daring deed he was about to pull with Price Waldrip drove everything else out of his mind—even the guilt pangs. A man like Price didn't pick up with every stray kid that came along. Living with Racker as he had, Harve realized dimly that he had lost a sense of his own worth. Price had done that much, awakened him to the fact that he was a person in his own right. It gave him a sense of power and dignity that was new to him.

Harve came to his feet at the sound of a horse on the bridge. The jay, silenced with the noise, winged over him, a flash of blue. Harve came to the edge of the hackberry bushes and watched Price's flashy black pick its way toward him.

Grinning, Price threw up his hand in greeting. "See you got 'em," he said, stepped down from the saddle, dropped his reins and clapped Harve on the shoulder with a rough hand. "Sure is nice havin' a buddy like you sidin' me, Harve."

Harve felt his chest swell with pride at unaccustomed praise. "Well, I done just like you said."

"Hard to find a pard who'll do that these days," Price declared. "Let's gather the remuda an' ride, buddy."

"How we going to do it, Price?" Harve asked.

"Come on," Price said. "I'll tell you about it while we ride."

On the wagon road, Price explained how it worked. "We find a place that's just right," he began, when they were walking their horses. "Generally speakin', it'll be a place on a grade, where they give the horses a breather. We take the box there but a few things we gotta do first." He furrowed his forehead in concentration.

"First thing, is to stake out our riding horses. That's for our getaway, Harve. I mind one time over in Idaho, I staked out *three* horses, 'bout twenty—thirty miles apart. I hit the bank in Montpelier, got out of town with the money bag with the sheriff and his posse right on my tail. I traded horses three times, and lost 'em easy as eatin' pie. I was in Utah before they knew what happened."

51

"A—a bank?"

Price laughed. "Yeah. That's where the money is, boy."

"I guess it is," Harve said feebly. He suddenly wished he could back out of this. He didn't want to rob a stagecoach. Or anything else. But old Price was depending on him. He couldn't let him down now. He had to go through with it— just this once, he promised himself. But that promise had a hollow sound. Once he went over the hump, pulled a gun on a man to make him do something, that was it. He'd be wanted by the law. There would be posters out on him. Peace officers all over the territory would have his picture or a description of him.

"You gotta keep your eyes open," Price was saying. "You look at things in the distance and you look again up close. You gotta know the lay of the land, Harve. That's how you come out on top in this business."

"How'd you get into it?"

"Well, it's a long story. Fella come through town where I lived with a string o' buckin' horses. He offered a real pretty silver-mounted saddle for anyone could ride a big, old tough outlaw. I rode him into the ground, Harve, and the fella wouldn't give me the saddle. I put a gun on him, Harve, and made him give it up. That's how I got started." He tugged his hat brim down down to eye level. "Anyway, that was my first job. That damn saddle turned green in about a week. Wasn't silver at all." He laughed.

The horses labored up the grade and Price reined in. "Just about here," he said with satisfaction. He stood in his stirrups, pointing back the way they'd come. "When we see that big old butte down there, you'll know we're nigh on this spot. Right here is where we'll take it from them, Harve. An' the pickin's ought to be good. There's a sawmill up at Jemez Springs and the Golden Glory mine and that strong-box'll have the payroll for both of 'em. We ought to make enough on this haul for both us to turn out to pasture if we want."

Don't go through with it, something warned him. He asked

nervously, "How you know the stage stops here to rest the horses?"

Price laughed. "That's easy. You can see where the horses been standin', Harve. An' it's wider here, the road, that is, so the driver can pull out in case another rig comes along."

"Yeah, I didn't notice."

"That's what you gotta train yourself to do," Price admonished in a kind voice. "You gotta see everything, Harve. Don't miss nothin'." He stared at Harve. "You do and you'll wind up eatin' trail dust every time."

He dismounted and took the lead rope from Harve and led out up a narrow draw. "Bring our horses," he said. He tethered the two led animals and took the burlap sacks from their backs.

Harve followed Price up the draw, leading the black and his roan. They climbed away from the road until Price found a gully deep enough to conceal the horses from anyone passing on the road. He tied them securely.

"Leave the saddles on . . . just loosen the cinches," he ordered, when Harve began unsaddling.

Price opened the burlap sacks and shook out the hay it held. There was enough hay to keep the horses going for a spell. Water seeped from the rocks and, by clearing out a space under the seep, it would fill and permit the animals to drink.

All this finished and Price looked around and then jerked his head toward the road and turned in that direction. Harve followed, excitement blazing inside him. This was all part of the business and while it was commonplace enough the illegality of it made it seem dangerous.

Back on the road, Price vaulted atop one of the horses Harve had rented from the livery and reined it around by the lead rope which he'd looped through the hackamore. "Let's ride, buddy," he said in the way that Harve liked to hear.

Harve mounted and they started off at once, following the road they'd taken on the way to staking out the horses.

They rode at a trot and Price talked about some of his escapades. It made dandy listening and almost before Harve realized it they were approaching Rowel.

Price halted on the town side of the bridge. He slipped to the ground. "Leave the road here, Harve, wait out there in the hackberries out of sight 'til about dusky-dark. Then take the horses back to the livery. I'll meet you at the Chuckwagon and we'll tie on the feedbag."

"You gonna walk into town?"

"Yep, it's just a little piece. So long, partner."

He struck out down the road, walking with long strides. Just before he disappeared, he turned, threw up his hand, and grinned.

Harve who'd been thinking about skedaddling back to Racker's was torn apart. First, he'd decide to do it and then change his mind. His indecision made him sick at his stomach. He sat the horse, holding the lead rope, his stomach tight as a knot.

Oh, Lordy, he thought, *what'm I gonna do?*

Suddenly he heard a sharp cry off beyond the hackberry bushes. It was the sound of a woman in distress.

VIII

HARVE DROPPED the lead rope, slipped from the horse and went down off the road quickly but without making any noise. Parting the brush he saw a man struggling with a girl. She was fighting to get away and not having any luck.

Harve ran forward. "Let her go!" he said. "Go on now, turn her loose!" He was outraged that a woman was fighting with a man.

The man, a little taller than Harve, swung his head, startled at this interruption. He wore range clothes, a ragged brush jacket and faded Levi's. A reddish stubble covered his face. The two guns on his legs were tied down with leather thongs. His teeth bared in what might have been a smile.

54

The girl, she wasn't a woman really, took the chance to jump away from the man, straightening her black hair. She was thin as a rail and her gray eyes were near big as goose eggs.

"What the dickens you trying to do?" Harve demanded hotly.

The man frowned. "Maybe you don't know who I am, sonny."

"I don't give a doodly dang who you are," Harve said, fighting the urge to swing on the man. "The lady hollered for help and that's all there is to it."

The man leaned forward, his hands hovering over the butts of the pistols. "You're buyin' yourself a mess o' trouble," the ginger-haired man said. "I'm Wes Carney. Maybe you didn't know that and now you run along while you're still able to hold water in your belly."

Oh dammit, thought Harve, *why didn't I get my gun out before I jumped in here with both feet?* He didn't believe he could match draws with a jasper who looked like a gunfighter.

Harve spoke with a calmness he didn't feel.

"You make a move for them guns and you'll be the late Wes Carney," he said. "You go on about your business and we'll call it even."

"Say, you talk like you might be able to use that hog-leg." Carney sneered. "Well, buster, it's your move."

"*No, no no!*" the girl whispered.

Carney took two steps forward and, with a sickness in his stomach, Harve jumped him, holding a wrist in each hand, while he bulled ahead, wrapping his legs around Carney's legs and the weight of his plunge threw the gunman on his back. Harve jerked out the guns and tossed them away. He kept hitting Carney with his fists as the man, cursing, struggled to his feet.

Wes Carney might be good with a gun but he didn't know anything about fist fighting. He backed away, covering his head with his arms, while Harve swarmed after him, hammering home savage blows.

A solid right landed on Carney's jaw and he went down like a wet saddle blanket. Harve leaped on him, hammering at him in a blind rage. He found the girl pulling at him.

"Please, don't, please, you'll kill him!"

He looked unseeingly at her but gradually the red mist cleared and he saw her face close to his. There was a little sprinkle of freckles on her nose. Her gray eyes were smoky and big with fright.

"Oh, but your face is bloody!"

"That's his blood," Harve declared, struggling to his feet. He wiped his face on his sleeve. "Come on, let's get out of here before he comes to. I don't want to pistol fight with him."

He went ahead of her and retrieved the horses. "I guess you wouldn't want to ride one of these plugs, no saddle or nothing."

"I walked out," she said. "I guess I can walk back."

"How come you're out here like this all alone?" he asked, a grim note in his voice.

"I arrived in Rowel, just a while ago," she said. "The stage is laying over until tomorrow. I walked out to try and ease my aches and pains from that long ride. That man followed me and—and—" She stopped on that note, blushing. "Thank you for saving me."

"It's all right," Harve said. "Anybody would have done the same. I'm Harvey Holley. I—I live down the road a piece."

"I'm Betsy Morrow," she said and offered him a slim brown hand.

Harve took her hand, the warmth of her palm giving him a funny feeling. "Well, Miss Morrow, you can't be too careful about skedaddlin' around in the brush out here in this wild country. If it's not men like Wes Carney it'd be a wild bull or maybe a big old mountain cat, like as not."

She glanced apprehensively around and moved closer

56

to him, an act that endeared her to him enormously, for some reason he could not understand. He laughed self-consciously. "Well, maybe not as bad as it sounds."

She shivered. "That man, Wes Carney. He—he's an evil person. You better watch out for him, Mister Holley."

"Whoa, there," he said, "I don't know who you're talking about, calling me 'mister.' Whyn't you call me Harve like evverybody else?"

"I will. If you'll call me Betsy."

"That's a deal, Betsy."

He'd never had much to do with girl critters but this one appeared to be all wool and a yard wide. He liked the way she walked along beside him with a swinging gait that wasn't sissified at all.

"What'll your folks think about you coming out here all by yourself?"

A shadow crossed her face. "I haven't any folks," she said. "That's why I'm traveling, Harve, going to live with an uncle of mine at Jemez Springs."

Good Lordy, thought Harve, *she's gonna be on that stage me and Price is gonna stick up!* He swallowed. "When you leaving Rowel?" he asked in a dry, cracked voice.

"Why, when the stage does," she said, glancing at him with a puzzled smile. "Gee Harve, you look kind of white. Are you all right?"

"Why, yes, I reckon to be all right," he said and plodded along in silence, all the joy gone out of his adventure.

He left her at the hotel and then walked the horses back to the livery. It was during the supper hour and no one was on duty in the stable and he was glad of it. He turned the animals into the corral and pitched in some hay. From there, he climbed the stairs to the room he shared with Price where he washed his face and hands and combed his hair.

He went down to the Chuckwagon and looked through the window. Price wasn't there so Harve waited around outside.

Price came out of the night so quietly Harve didn't see him until the big man spoke.

"How'd it go, Harve boy?"

Startled, Harve wheeled. "Fine as silk, real fine."

"Well, let's go inside and get a load o' grub," Price said heartily and moved toward the open door of the Chuckwagon.

"Wait a minute, Price," Harve said quietly.

Something in his voice made Waldrip stop short and wheel. "What is it, Harve?" he asked shortly.

"Look, Price, maybe we better hold off until the next stage. Let's not hit this one, buddy."

"How come?" Price leaned his head toward Harve as though to see him better in the gloom. "What you got on your mind, Harve?"

Forcing a laugh, Harve said "Just a hunch, Price. I just got a feeling, that's all."

Price hit him on the shoulder with his palm. "Get shet o' that feelin', buddy boy," he said briskly. "We done staked out the getaway horses and everything. We back out now we might not get another chance. Come on, get a big steak under them skinny ribs and you'll feel a sight better."

He took Harve's arm and pulled him along.

Harve resisted. "No, I mean it, Price. We better get the next one."

Price moved in close and his fingers closed on Harve's arm like a steel trap. "Listen, boy, that's the only stage that carries that kind of money see? We don't get that one, it'll be a month from now before we get another chance." He looked at Harve and then, laughing, relaxed his grip on Harve's arm. "You see, we gotta get this'n, buddy, because old Price is about to run out o' the long green, too." He wheeled away, not waiting for Harve to answer.

Harve stood there for a long moment, thinking bleakly, *you done good, but not good enough. You better come up with a reason to get back to that ranch and do it quick.*

But nothing came to him. He followed Price slowly into the Chuckwagon; but he knew he wasn't going to enjoy his supper.

IX

HARVEY HOLLEY walked out of the Grand Central's bar and leaned against the whitewashed boards of the front wall, running the back of his hand across his mouth as he'd seen Price do. He didn't want to go on but there didn't seem to be much else to do. His heart was like a blacksmith's anvil and he was half afraid it meant he was a coward.

Leaning against the wall he studied the big stage in front of the hotel, dusty but shining where someone had rubbed a hand over the fancy gold lettering that said, *Butterfield Stage.* Across the street two riders were tying in at the mercantile and a laundry wagon was hitched in front of Emily Clutt's new steam laundry. The story of Marshal Bill Pelley's chase of old Toby Lamb's killer was the topic of the day. No one had heard from the marshal since he'd rode off alone in pursuit of the Chinaman.

Harve felt the hard slow beat of his heart under his purple shirt, and the rising excitement drove away some of his misgiving. *Heck,* he thought, *I'll never see that freckle-faced gal again and it won't make no difference, none at all.* He kept saying that but it seemed to make him all the more reluctant.

He glanced at the louvered doors. Price Waldrip was behind those swinging doors and Price had picked him for a partner. Harve's shirt tightened against the buttons with the swell of his chest. He dropped his hand to the Colt on his hip and brushed it deeper into the holster, turning his attention to the stage, trying not to think of old man Racker for a moment.

The driver went past Harve, belching easily, and stood by the front wheel looking ahead to the four fairly well-matched grays restlessly shaking bridle chains and moving their slick, rounded rumps in nervous anticipation of the haul toward Jemez Springs. The driver was a tall, gaunt man with gray eyes and a brown face as wrinkled as a prune. He looked over at Harve and closed one eye and took a plug of twist from his hip pocket and gnawed at it. He replaced the plug and bent to take up two links on the trace chain of the near wheeler. He went around the horses, inspecting each of them, circling, and returned to stand by the front wheel. He used the toe of his boot to wipe a nob of black grease from the hub and then kicked his boot against a spoke to dislodge it. For some unaccountable reason, Harve felt touched by these homely movements, making his own intentions seem evil and unreal.

He won't put up no fight, Harve thought hopefully, *none at all.*

But you can't be sure, a warning voice from somewhere added.

The shotgun guard came out next and the driver held the Greener while the guard climbed to the boot.

Harve breathed deep when the guard reached down and took the double-barreled, sawed-off shotgun and settled himself on the seat.

The passengers came straggling out of the hotel and stood around the stage. Betsy Morrow didn't see him as she mounted the stage with a flash of white-clad ankle. In broad daylight she seemed even thinner and more freckled, and below the little flat yellow hat with flowers and ribbons on it, her black hair gleamed.

A bowler-topped man wearing a checkered vest followed and then an older man with a couple of white horns of mustache, black-hatted and frock-coated.

Harve brought his shoulder away from the wall. He felt sweat form on his forehead and roll down over his face. He swiped his sleeve across his forehead and settled his hat back in place. The trace of coming leanness in his face was overshadowed with grim fatality. His blue eyes were unnaturally bright. He put down the sudden feathery fright lance that speared his innards. He repressed his fright by thinking, *I'm not eighteen and here I'm pulling a job with Price Waldrip.* A small, inner voice asked another question: *What about Racker, Harve, all alone out there on the ranch? What about him? Yeah, and what about the girl?*

There was still time to run.

At that moment Price pushed out of the Grand Central. He stopped beside Harve and pushed his elbow gently into Harve's ribs and said: "See that filly get on, Harve?" Looking at Harve, he grinned wickedly, his teeth flashing beneath the black mustache that was so carefully curled. "Quite a piece there, eh Harve?" He didn't lower his voice and drew a sharp look of disapproval from the driver.

Waldrip's elbow dug even deeper into Harve's ribs as two men, straining under the weight of the strongbox, took short steps from the Wells Fargo office toward the stage. Waldrip's black eyes took on a shine as the box was muscled up into the boot where the driver could rest his feet on it.

How in the world we gonna take that thing with us? Harve thought in desperation. *Must weigh a ton!* He glanced at Waldrip and his heart dropped to his worn boots.

Price was like a steer being branded, red lips parted, black eyes glistening.

"Tie it down good," the driver drawled. "I don't wanna hafta stop a mile outta town and do it all over."

"Hank, you do too much worryin'," one of the men drawled back. "All you gotta do is haul it. We done the totin'."

"We better tote it all the way t' Golden Glory," the other helper said. "I doubt this here so-called whip can get it t' there in one piece."

"All set, Harve?" Waldrip asked in a soft voice.

Harve swallowed and nodded, following Price to the stage. He saw the tails of Waldrip's coat lift over the black-handled Colt and he felt another surge of fright. He wanted to turn and run like a coyote but he didn't. He climbed into the stage and squeezed in beside Price. The girl sat across from him and her knees almost touched his own. She kept her eyes on her hands folded in her lap. Harve was in an agony, waiting for her to notice him.

Price leaned forward and asked in a polite but suggestive voice, "Comfortable, miss?"

The girl made a brief nod without looking up.

There were cheery shouts from the spectators as the stage readied to depart. The driver swung his whip and its pistol-like crack split the quiet of Main Street. Looking out the side window, Harve saw the laundry wagon horse jump as the whip popped. The stage jerked away, the box swaying crazily in its leather cradle. There was a creak and a jangle, and the hollow cluck-cluck of well-greased wheels, as the four powerful horses moved smoothly down Main Street and set up their racket crossing Pitch Creek bridge.

Price leaned closer to the girl and asked, "Where you goin', ma'am?"

She kept her eyes on her hands and Harve agonizedly wondered why Price didn't leave her alone. It was plain to see that she didn't want to talk to Price. For some reason it gave him pleasure.

Betsy's lips moved minutely.

"What's that, ma'am?" Price asked.

A hot anger burned Harve but he kept his mouth shut with an effort. He watched the girl's face, saw the tiny line of brown freckles marching across her nose, like a sprinkle of bran. *Why you worrying about a freckle-faced gal for?* Harve asked himself. *There's a bigger worry out at Racker's place—where you ought to be right now.*

Betsy spoke louder. "To Jemez Springs."

"Jemez Springs' gain, some other town's loss," the frock-coated man said in a full, preacher-throated voice.

"Yeah. Yes, sir." Waldrip grinned.

The man with the checkered vest looked at Harve. "Not sick are you, son?" he asked with concern.

"No," Harve said. "I ain't sick." He wiped his forehead with the palm of his hand and it came away wet.

When he spoke Betsy looked at him for the first time. She smiled pleasurably and said in a glad voice: "Harve!"

"Hi," Harve said.

Price gave Harve a sharp and speculative look and then, satisfied, turned his attention to the girl. "Right long ride," he said. "I'll try an' keep you from bein' lonesome."

The frock-coated man frowned at Price. He cleared his throat authoritatively and said "Mister, don't you reckon this lady don't need yo 'entertainment."

Price's grin disappeared. A vein in his forehead throbbed as he swung his head and his black eyes narrowed. "You keep shut, old man, I need your he'p I'll let you know."

The man's throat worked visibly. He made an immediate decision. "Just as you say, suh," he said.

X

As THE STAGE rocked along, Harve's conscience took over. He kept remembering Racker, alone and helpless at the ranch. Harve knew that Racker liked him . . . and he sort of liked Racker, too, in spite of having to cater to him. It didn't help when he told himself it'd be this one job, to pay Racker back, and that would be the end of it. Somehow he sensed that he'd reached a fork in the road and he was taking the wrong turn, powerless to stop.

He looked covertly at Betsy. He wondered what she'd think if she knew that he and Price meant to hold up the stage. That was the first time he'd put it in plain, unvarnished thought and it seemed even more shockingly unreal, even impossible. He'd never done anything like this, not even in his thoughts.

The stage stopped at Cruces to change horses. The passengers got out to stretch and Harve found himself apart from the group with Betsy. *Like two strays bunching together,* he thought. "I'm sorry, Betsy, my friend is kind of fresh."

"That's all right. I'm used to it."

Somehow that made him angry. "It's not all right," he said fiercely and she looked at him in surprise.

"Well, what I mean—where'd you say you goin'?" He remembered well enough but he was embarrassed at his outburst.

"To Jemez Springs. To my uncle's. I'm going to live with him." She glanced at him. "You remember, I told you. . ."

"Yeah, I remember. You all alone except for that uncle?" She nodded.

Awkwardly, he said, "I ain't got nobody either."

"I'm sorry." She lifted her head. "My paw was a stage driver. The stage was held up about a month ago. The road agent shot him."

"Gee whiz," Harve whispered. "That was bad." With a sudden shock he realized something like that might happen. He looked at the tobacco-chewing driver, watching his new team being hitched to the stage. Harve's knees shook with the thought that he might be shooting at that man before long.

Betsy peered at him anxiously. "You all right? You're so pale—"

"Sure, sure, I'm all right," he murmured confusedly. "All right, I guess." He shoved his hands in his pockets. "How 'bout you? Think you'll like Jemez Springs?"

To his surprise tears flooded her eyes. She turned her back on him. "I'm sorry," she said in a choked voice. "I really am. I'm so scared, Harve. I don't want to go but there isn't any other place. I have to go." She did something with a little bit of lacy handkerchief and when she turned around her face was steady, her eyes dry. "Excuse me, please," she said, and smiling, brightly asked: "What do you do, Harve?"

He felt all choked up around the gullet. Here was a girl with a heap of grit. "I work for a man named Racker," he said. "Sort of ramrod his spread." *It wasn't a lie,* he thought defensively. He was the whole kit and caboodle of Racker's crew.

Wide-eyed with admiration, she said, "You're awfully young to have such a responsible job."

"Goin' on eighteen."

"Well, you're a couple years older than me." Betsy said.

"All right, folks!" the driver hollered and the passengers straggled out of the rest station. The driver slammed the door shut and the stage moved on its leather springs as the man climbed to his seat. The vehicle moved off with a series of pops from the driver's whip and profanity.

Price had had a drink in the rest station. His elbow found Harve's ribs again and he whispered, "Makin' time, hey boy?"

Brice's whisper filled the stage despite the noise. Harve's ears burned. The girl stopped smiling and bent her head, looking at her clasped hands. She didn't look at him again.

Dang that Price Waldrip, Harve thought with fury.

The noisy stage rocked on through the heat and dust, crossing hot gray Ute Mesa and entered the canyon. Harve, looking out the stage window, recognized the terrain. There was the butte that Waldrip had pointed out. The stage was nearing the turnout.

His throat was dry. The stage slowed to a crawl as the grade steepened and roughened. The sound of the whip made Harve flinch inside. Not long now, the horses were tied up just a short distance ahead.

Then it would happen. He'd become an outlaw, a ridge-rider, always on the dodge. The security of Racker's place seemed suddenly remote, something he'd never known.

Price Waldrip changed somehow. His dark eyes narrowed and held a cruel, unremitting look heightened by the thinned lips. Perspiration beaded his dark forehead. He was suddenly restless, moving constantly, looking from one side to the other.

The air grew heavy inside the stage.

"Somethin' botherin' you?" the man in the checkered vest asked in a friendly voice.

"Not a damn thing," Waldrip said as the stage jolted to a halt.

Harve saw that the driver had pulled into the turnout. He felt like vomiting.

Waldrip stepped over the frock-coated man's feet and got to the ground. Harve emerged on the other side, taking in, in a single glance, the whole picture. The guard was on his knees, placing a big rock behind the rear wheel to keep the stage from rolling backward while the horses took a breather. Probably the brakes were not too good.

Harve saw the gun in Waldrip's hand as in a dream, the look of surprise that washed across the guard's face and his sudden glance toward the Greener, standing with its short muzzle leaned against a boulder beside the road.

"No trouble," Waldrip said softly. "No trouble at all, mister." He glanced up at the driver. "Throw it down, mister."

The driver bent, struggling, his face reddening with effort. The box thudded to the ground.

"Don't stand there, boy," Waldrip said, an edge to his voice. "Get it on your shoulder! Wait—unhook the horses first."

Harve had his gun in his hand. He moved as though in a trance, obeying Waldrip's command to take out the horses.

"Come on, gal, get out of there," Waldrip said to Betsy.

Harve stopped beside the rear wheel, looking across at Price Waldrip. "No," he said. "No, Price, I—"

"Hell, they can pick her up across the next hill," Waldrip said in disgust. "Come on, gal, get out."

"No!" Harve shouted in sudden rage.

Price Waldrip cursed him, a rapid, fluent string of seasoned words and it ended as abruptly as it began. He simply pointed his gun at Harve.

Harve threw himself aside as Waldrip's gun flamed. He yelled: "Don't!" in a high, thin voice and fired his own gun and through the spokes of the front wheel he saw Waldrip's legs buckle.

The horses snorted and moved uneasily while the driver held them in.

Price went to his knees, his mouth slack and he tried to grab a spoke of the wheel to hold himself up. His hand slipped from the spoke and he fell heavily on his side.

Harve stared, his chest full and a lump in his throat. His eyes felt hot and blurry. *I got to get out of here. To heck with that strongbox. I don't want it nohow.*

He turned his gun toward the driver and let it drift to the guard. "Don't none of you move," he warned and stepped off the road. He scrambled up the gully, his heart hammering in his chest. Behind him he heard shouting but he didn't wait. There was a kind of numbness in him and a sickness, too. What he wanted to see most of all was the horses he and Price had staked out.

He rounded a big rock and paused. The horses were there. He heard shouting again from the road and it was like a push toward his horse. He immediately decided that he'd strip the saddle and bridle from Price's horse and turn it loose.

He reached the roan and quickly tightened the cinches. He whirled at a slight sound behind him, drawing his gun as he turned.

Betsy Morrow stood there staring at him with frightened eyes. Her little yellow hat was flopped to one side and a smear of dirt smudged one cheek.

"What're you doin' here?" he snapped.

She looked him steadily in the eye. "I'm going with you!" she said.

XI

BURT RACKER was near out of his mind when Harvey didn't return. In his guilt-ridden mind the old man had imagined every possible reason why Harve, the dependable one, hadn't returned from town; all of the reasons had to do with the black-eyed stranger.

A wandering pair of range tramps came on the Double

H and after feeding them, an unusual occurrence, Racker gave them five dollars to ride across the near ridge to Jess Sykes' place, the nearest neighbor, and deliver a note. In the note Racker asked Sykes to drive him to Rowel, promising to pay him for his trouble.

That was how Racker entered Rowel on the day the stage left for Jemez Springs. In fact, Sykes had pulled his team off the road to let the stage pass. Racker hadn't even raised up from the bed of the high-seated spring wagon that carried most of Sykes' belongings when the stage rattled past.

Sykes was leaving the country. "What with a bunch of hungry redskins prowlin', I've had enough," he said briefly as his two long-legged sons helped load Racker on a pallet his wife had made. They set out for town. The two boys walked behind the wagon. The range tramps, Crick Justan and Spade Cooley, rode behind the boys, lazing in their saddles and speculating on Racker's indisposition.

In town, Racker made inquiries from his sick bed in the wagon before the marshal's office. The marshal was off chasing a crazy Chinaman, he was told, and the sheriff was at the capital, witnessing against a man who'd killed that homesteader family on Lincoln Creek.

Sykes twisted around in the seat, staring at Racker, as a crowd gathered around the wagon. "What you want to do, Burt?"

"Dunno," Racker said, groaning. "I'm a sick man, Jess, an' that's a fact. Dunno what to do."

Purvis, the banker, seeing the crowd, came over and peered into the wagon. "Racker, what's up?"

"Lookin' for that fool kid," Racker said, groaning again.

"He's took up with a no-good," Purvis snapped. "I chased him all over Hades and half of town, trying to collect your note money. He's slippery as a sidewinder, that one. Never did catch up to him."

Racker let out a piteous groan. "Did—did he take off with that big black-headed feller?"

"The same," Purvis said. "What you gonna do about your note, Burt?"

Racker had not borrowed the money because he needed it, but only to give the illusion of poverty. He forgot his original intention as he painfully put his hand inside his shirt and fumbled with the buttons on his money belt. He took out a sheaf of greenbacks and counted out the necessary amount.

Crick Justan and Spade Cooley exchanged glances as Purvis accepted the money with compressed lips and a promise to write him a receipt as soon as he got back to the bank.

Racker saw the two of them as he pulled himself upright. "You two boys lookin' for work?"

"Sure are, Mr. Racker," Crick said.

"Me and Crick sure'd admire to he'p you out," Spade chimed in. "What's the pay?"

"Forty and found," Racker grunted. "See if you can scare up a few more hands and come back here quick as you can."

The two men dismounted and tied their horses and began scouting for additional help. "You let me pick 'em," Crick said to Spade, as they headed for the town saloons.

"Mr. Racker, what you gonna do?" Sykes asked plaintively, anxious to be rid of his passenger.

"What're *you* gonna do?" Racker replied peevishly.

"Why get t' hell an' gone outta this country," Sykes said.

"Then sell me your team and spring wagon," Racker said. "I'll have one o' them new hands o' mine drive me back home."

Sykes looked at his silent wife while his two sons looked on open-mouthed.

"You'll need a team and wagon where we light," Mrs. Sykes said. After more moves than she could keep track of, she was beginning to think they'd never find the right place.

Sykes nodded. "But we can buy another. Cheaper than what Racker'll pay for this'n."

She leaned closer to whisper: "He's crazy as a bed bug. Throwin' money around like it comes off trees."

"That's his lookout." Sykes twisted in his seat. "You kin have the team and wagon," he said, "for six hundred cash money."

"Done," Racker said and began counting out the money.

On the return trip to the Double H, Spade Cooley drove carefully, to avoid the worst bumps. Every time the wheel hit a rock or dropped in a hole, Racker grunted or groaned.

Behind the wagon, Crick Justan rode at the head of four hardcase characters he'd picked up in the town saloons. Crick was more excited than he'd been in a long, long time. This old coot was really loaded. Crick was more than pleased at how things were turning out. If he and Spade worked it right they just might be able to get together enough scratch to start a ranch of their own. He grunted with pleassure at the sudden thought: *We might even get the old man's spread. He looks like he's not long for this world.*

Even Racker felt better than he appeared. *Let 'em come,* he thought, *they'll get a reception they won't forget.* Every single one of his new hands appeared to know what a pistol was for and how to use it.

Marshal Bill Pelley, by hard riding, came on the Rowel-to-Jemez Springs stagecoach as the driver, guard and passengers ringed the dying outlaw. He dismounted and pushed his way to Price Waldrip and knelt beside the man.

Waldrip's black eyes were open, clouded with pain. But he grinned and said, "You didn't take as long as I thought you would."

"What's it all add up to, Price?" Pelley asked.

"That kid Harve, he—" Waldrip stopped speaking and red bubbles appeared on his lip. His eyes glazed and he stared unseeingly at the sky.

Rising, Pelley looked around at the ring of solemn faces.

"Where's Harvey?" he asked, dusting the knees of his pants.

They all started talking at once and he held up his hand. "One at a time," he said patiently.

The driver spat. "We'd just stopped the team for a rest on the grade. That feller throwed down on me and made me dump the box. He was fixin' to take the gal, too. Harve said 'no' and they shot it out. Harve high-tailed up the gully there."

"The gal followed him," the guard put in. "I yelled at her t' come back. She kept a-goin'."

"How'd you get here so fast, Marshal?"

Pelley heaved a deep sigh and rubbed his jaw. "Waldrip killed old Tobe and scared off the Chinaman. Just to get me out o' town, I reckon. Soon as I got the lay from the Chinaman, I high-tailed it back to Rowel. 'Course, soon's I got there, I found Waldrip had took the stage and I figured what he had on his mind. I got a fresh horse and took a short cut or two."

"Marshal, you near made it," the driver said. "Well, if you got no objection, I got to get this rig to Jemez Springs sometime today."

"Go right ahead," Pelley said. "Me, I got to track that young hellion."

"Wonder why that gal took off thataway?" the driver wondered aloud.

Pelley shrugged and picked up his reins, thinking he'd like the answer to that, along with a lot of other answers to questions puzzling him. The hard riding hadn't done much to improve on Pelley's good nature. *None of it made sense,* he thought coldly. He'd have to catch Harve to find out what went on and his rancor at the youngster was like a taste of gall in his throat.

"Looky here, Betsy," Harve argued, sitting his horse and looking down into her upturned face, "sure I'd like to have you but it's plain crazy. I'm gonna be on the run. No place out here for a girl."

"I won't be any trouble," she promised in a soft, pleading voice. "I'd rather do anything in the world than go to Uncle Wendel's. I don't even know him."

"Give him a chance," Harve said. "Hurry now, before that stage takes off. They won't wait long." He was terrified at the thought of being responsible for Betsy. He had enough trouble on his hands without a girl along to mess things up. He yearned horribly to be back in the placid life he led before his encounter with Price Waldrip. He shivered at the thought of the man and was seized by guilt feelings again. He'd never shot a man before, and the experience made him sick to his stomach, just remembering Price falling to the ground, grabbing at that spoke.

"I won't go back," she said in a low but determined voice.

Reluctantly, he dismounted and tightened the cinches on the nervous black and helped her up. She had trouble with the folds of her dress but finally got most of it tucked under 'her leg. She straightened the little hat and said in a small voice, "I'm ready."

Harve felt like crying but he grunted, mounted and led out, up and away from the road, heading for the distant folds of the mountain where he might feel secure. He had no idea what he'd do and the lack of a plan depressed him. *Can't let that girl know I'm scared witless,* he thought dully. *Got to put on a face of sorts.*

He looked back. She held to the horn with both hands, clinging like a dude. The little yellow hat had skewed to one side again and her black hair was tangled. He shook his head in despair. What in the world would happen to them? Why did she latch on to him?

They came out of a shallow coulee opening on a bench where other canyons fanned out. He stopped and gazed across the maze of canyons ridging the land. Rough country, all of it. He knew it well. An occasional trapper cruised the streams looking for beaver. Lone prospectors prowled the hills searching for their personal bonanza. Lonely outlaw trails ending at some robber's roost crisscrossed the savage and lonely land. He shook his head despairingly. How could he manage with a girl?

He looked at the object of his misery and found that she was looking at him with a question mark in her eyes.

"Where are we going?" she asked.

"Danged if I know," he confessed. "Circle north and hide our tracks well as we can. Come up the valley between Jemez and the Sangres. Keep out o' sight and hope for the best."

"Why north?"

"Well, after Jemez Springs, there's not much for a long, long piece. Anybody taking out after us would figure we'd head south toward some of the settlements."

"You haven't done anything. Why should you fear pursuit?"

Harve said nothing and Betsy pressed. "Well, have you?"

"I can't say that tryin' to stick up a stage is nothing."

"But you didn't take anything," she insisted.

"That doesn't matter. Anyway, there's this other thing." He was quiet for a long time and then he began talking, telling her about how he'd sold Racker's horses and gambled the money away. He didn't spare himself, even telling her in a sweat of self-recrimination that he'd let Racker down by not paying off the note. "Maybe they'll throw the old man off'n the place," he finished.

She was silent and then straightening, she pointed below.

Harve twisted in the saddle and looked in the direction she indicated, a tingle of dread spearing him. "Pelley!"

"Who's that?" she asked.

Angered at her and himself, he snapped: "Just the marshal, that's all. Bill Pelley. And he's on *my* trail. Let's get out of here." He touched the roan with spurs and led out, heading for rocky ground that wouldn't leave a trace of their passing. "Git!" He urged the horse on faster than good sense allowed.

The rise of the land soon hid Pelley but the sense of being pursued didn't leave him. He pushed his horse hard, taking a perverse pleasure in Betsy's efforts to keep close to him. He waited on her more and more often. She was far behind, screened by a turn in the canyon they were following when he heard the harsh command:

"Reach for the sky, sonny!"

XII

HARVE recognized the man as Wes Carney. He held a gun pointed at Harve as he rode out from between two rocks, followed by two slouchy, dirty men in range clothes. There was a puzzled look on Carney's brush-covered face.

"Where's the black-headed feller?" he demanded.

Harve shook his head, unable to answer for the dryness in his throat. He told himself he wasn't afraid but he wasn't very convincing.

"Well, come on, I ast you where he's at?" Carney said, brandishing his pistol.

"He—he got shot."

Carney threw a startled look at his two companions. "Shot? Did them dirty stinkin' coyotes—" He stopped speaking and his eyes narrowed as he coldly studied Harve. "Where's the payroll, buster?"

"Yeah, where at is all that do re me?" This was the squint-eyed man with the ragged cinnamon-colored hair.

"Shut up, Squint," Carney grated.

"Don't know nothing about the money," Harve said, praying that Betsy would keep to cover.

"You better start talking, kid," Carney grated. "Think it over. I'll give you another minute or two."

"Aw, Wes, shoot him in the belly," Squint said. "He'll talk with his guts spillin' out."

"I told you the truth. I know nothing about the payroll."

Carney moved his knees, urging his horse closer. "I know all about it, button, so don't pull no savvy on me see? I'm giving you a break kid. Just tell me where the money is and I'll let you go."

"I–"

Harve didn't get a chance to complete another denial. Betsy rode around an outcropping and all eyes swung to her.

"Well, well, well," Carney said, his eyes going near shut as he licked his lips. He glanced at Harve with triumph. "Looks like we done hit the jackpot, boys."

Betsy wheeled her horse and kicked the animal in the ribs but Squint spurred ahead and grabbed the black's bridle. He hauled the animal up so sharply, it reared, and Betsy spilled to the ground.

Harve dismounted and, kneeling beside her, raised her from the ground. She looked at him dazedly, unseeing.

"You hurt?" he asked hoarsely. "You all right, Betsy?"

At the mention of her name she shook her head two or three times and her eyes returned to fucus.

"Just shook up, that's all," she said in a whisper.

Harve helped her to her feet and she leaned weakly against him. The three men encircled them with their horses.

Wes Carney said, "Where's the money this kid took off the stage?"

Betsy regarded him steadily even though Harve could feel her trembling. "He didn't take anything," she said.

"What's this about Price getting shot?"

"That's right, he did get shot," Betsy said. "Harve shot him in self-defense."

That startled look crossed Carney's face again. He reared back in the saddle, his mouth turning down. "Harve shot him?" he echoed. He turned a black look on Harve. "What'd you do that for?" he demanded. "Didn't you–" He stopped short, looking at his two companions.

All of them dismounted. "You hold horses, Dingus," Carney said, "and watch these two."

Carney and Squint approached them while Dingus held

75

the horses. "Gonna tie you up," Carney said. "While we make a palaver."

"Don't tie her up," Harve said. "She ain't going no place."

"We gonna make sure," Carney said. "Turn around, boy, and put your wrists together behint yore back."

Harve stepped in front of Betsy. "I said, don't tie her up," he said boldly.

Carney was still holding his pistol in his hand. He simply slammed it against Harve's head.

It was like an explosion in his brain. He found himself on his hands and knees on the ground. He heard Betsy cry out and then felt a boot slam into his ribs, knocking him flat on the ground.

A groan forced its way past his throat and he felt warm blood running down his cheek.

His hands were roughly bound while he lay helpless and then he was propped against a rock. He could feel Betsy close to him, trying to cradle his head.

"Look out," he croaked, "you'll get blood all over you."

Her hands had been tied in front of her body and she used a tiny handkerchief to staunch the flow of blood that came from the blow on his head.

"What they got to palaver about?" he wondered aloud in a weak voice.

"I don't know," she whispered as though afraid of being overheard. The three men squatted a dozen feet away, talking in low voices. "I'm afraid, Harvey."

He put confidence he didn't feel into his voice. "Don't," he said. "We'll be all right. Pelley'll be along directly."

"So he shot Price," Squint said. "What d' y think o' that, the stinkin' kid. What we gonna do now, Wes?"

"We goin' on with the job on old man Racker?" Dingus wanted to know.

"You're dang tootin' we are. I ain't passin' up fifty thousand frogskins just becuz Price is gone. I know the plan an' we kin do it easy."

"Mebbe the ol' man ain't really got it," Dingus said doubtfully.

"Look, Price done checked all that out. That ol' man's still got the first nickel he ever owned. We just gotta make him tell us where it is. He knows Harve is with us it'll be easy to sweat it out o' him."

"But Harve ain't with us," Dingus said with blunt logic.

"He will be when I get through with that gal," Wes said viciously. "I got a couple marks ag'in that rooster—after we get the loot." He had too much pride, such as it was, to tell his buddies how Harve had taken his guns from him and knocked him out. He had resisted the urge to shoot Harve down, the moment he laid eyes on him, for one reason alone: Harve could prove useful.

The blowing of a horse faintly reached them and they reacted animal-like, springing to their feet, drawing guns, their faces turned in the direction of the sound. Wes Carney catfooted to a rock, removed his hat and peered over the top of the gray granite. He swore in a voice edged with fear.

"That damn marshal. Gimme my rifle, Squint. I'll fix his little red wagon."

Squint yanked the Winchester from the boot and hurried to hand Carney the rifle. Carney worked it quietly to keep the noise down and Harve saw the flash of brass as a cartridge was levered into the chamber.

He sucked in his breath and yelled: "Look out, Pelley, they gonna bushwhack you!"

The rifle blasted a fraction of a second after Harve yelled his warning. Cursing, Carney whirled and pointed the rifle at Harve. Betsy screamed.

"Don't shoot!" Squint warned. "Let's get outta here, Wes!"

Carney ran to Harve, raised the rifle and brought the butt down on his head, knocking him unconscious.

"Get 'em on hosses," he said. "We takin' 'em along."

Some time later Harve regained consciousness. He was lying bellydown across his saddle and his head throbbed like it held an Indian war drum. He was unable to stifle a groan.

At the sound of the groan the cavalcade stopped. Harve was sick, retching until his stomach hurt.

"Untie him," Betsy said. "Untie him this minute!"

Carney chuckled. "Feisty, aincha?" But he nodded to Dingus. "Go on, Dingus. Cut him loose."

Harve heard the creak of saddle leather and saw Dingus' boots. The knife touched his wrists and he would have fallen to the ground if Dingus hadn't grabbed him. The motion bloomed fresh pain in his head and for a moment the world whirled around him. Dingus let him slide to the ground where he lay in a motionless heap, his hands pressed to his head.

He felt Betsy's hands on him, tenderly soft and careful. She helped him into a sitting position and whispered in his ear: "Pretend you're still sick. They might get careless."

"I don't have to pretend," he muttered. "I am." He pillowed his head in his hands. "Gosh, my head's got a hammer inside it." He sat that way for a moment, then looked at Betsy. "Where are we?" He looked past her at Dingus leaning against his horse, rolling a smoke and watching him. The other two sat their horses, talking in low voices.

Betsy shook her head. "I don't know. We must have lost the marshal. We're not hurrying as we did at first."

Harve surveyed the country, trying to pick out a landmark he would recognize and get his bearings. They were down at the bottom of a shallow canyon, on the edge of a grove of stunted cedars. Across a deep crevice the buckbrush grew thick and he saw nothing familiar, nothing that gave him a clue to their present location. *If I could climb that ol' peak over there,* he thought . . .

"Dingus, you scout around. We can make camp any time now," Carney said, looking at the westering sun with his hand shading his eyes. "Gonna be dark 'fore we know it."

Dingus mounted and rode out while Carney and Squint

dismounted. Carney came over and squatted beside Harve. "Think you can behave yourself now?" He grinned.

Harve closed his eyes.

"That ain't no answer. I hate to keep poundin' you but I ain't gonna let you get away, boy."

"What do you want?" Harve asked faintly.

"Well, now, that'll take a little talkin' about. You promise you won't try to slope out and I won't tie you up."

"What do you want from me?"

"Comes time and I'll tell y'all about it," Carney said. He rose as the sounds of a horseman came to them.

Carney relaxed as Dingus rode into view.

"Wes, they's a scabby bunch o' Injuns camped down by the crick," Dingus said. "Maybe a dozen."

"We'll go upstream and upwind," Carney said. "They ain't gonna bother us none. Not if'n it's that bunch we spotted day before yestiddy. Come on, let's get a move on 'fore it gets plumb dark."

Harve gritted his teeth and hung on to the saddle horn. The jolt of his horse didn't help his headache but he was curious now. It was plain to him that Carney had some plan in mind that he was carrying out. He cast around, trying to find a clue but his headache only got worse.

The sun was gone and the sky to the west was a blaze of pinks and golds when they came to the creek. Squint began gathering firewood but Carney stopped him.

"No fire," he said. "We'll make a dry camp and eat beans outta the can."

There was a protesting whine in Squint's voice. "I wanna cuppa coffee."

Carney considered and then nodded reluctantly. "Well, just a little fire. We'll douse it soon's the coffee boils." He glanced at Harve and Betsy. "You two sit down over there against that rock. No monkey business, mind you."

Harve and Betsy sat silently, watching Squint hunker over his small fire, feeding in bits of dry tinder. With the sun gone, a sudden chill came on them. Betsy moved closer

79

to Harve. He looked at her. Her hat was frazzled and the black hair was in disarray. A smudge of dirt was on one cheek.

She turned her head and her eyes met his. She smiled and he felt his heart swell. *This girl sure has a lot of spunk. That's for dang sure,* he told himself.

"Don't worry," he whispered, "everything's gonna turn out all right."

He didn't know how it could be made to turn out all right, but it had to when he saw the confident smile she gave him. It was just as though she suddenly let him know that she depended on him, believed in him, and he felt the load fall on his shoulders.

The night was black. The men hurried to get ready to bed down before dousing the fire. Squint brought their bedrolls. He tied Harve's feet together and then his hands and brought them down to his feet and made them secure.

Squint grinned at Harve. "You gonna be comfy," he said. Then he tied Betsy the same way. When they were both firmly bound, he spread both Harve's and Price's blankets over them and said softly, "Nighty night," and then roared at his humor.

"Funny, huh?" Harve muttered.

He was not too uncomfortable, lying on his side with his feet drawn up. He could turn over but he didn't because he was afraid he wouldn't be able to cover himself if the blanket fell off.

The fire hissed as Dingus emptied a coffeepot of water on it.

Harve lay there listening to the swiftly rushing creek, thinking about the hopelessness of their plight. Up on the ridge, a coyote barked sharply and, off in the distance, another answered.

He moved restlessly. He was tied tighter than the skin on a drum. His wrists were already raw from trying to jerk his hands through the coils of piggin string that held him. He knew he'd not be able to skin out of that rope.

But the rawhide was already wet with his sweat or blood, he didn't know which, and when it dried it'd shrink the rawhide. Squint had done a job of tying him up.

Carney spoke from his bedroll. "Better take them horses up the crick aways to a fresh patch o' grass."

"Aw, hell," Dingus whined. "I'm in my soogan, Wes."

"Me, too," Squint said in a sleepy voice.

"Well, dammit, one of you," Carney said menacingly.

"Listen, Squint—" Dingus began.

"No, you lis'n," Squint said savagely. "I get outta my bed I'm gonna kick hell outta you 'fore I get back in it."

"Oh, all right, dang it."

There were sounds in the night as Dingus began moving the horses to fresh grass. He stumbled in the darkness, cursing softly.

Harve considered. Dingus was the idiot of the outfit. Both Carney and Squint imposed on him, making him the butt of their rough jokes and their errand boy. Dingus might be tiring of the role. Harve listened intently and when he heard Dingus returning he waited until the man was near him, then whispered: "Dingus!"

Dingus halted and stood there.

Harve, reassured by snores from the mounds beyond where the fire had been, whispered again.

Dingus came near and bent over. "Whatcha want?" he asked suspiciously, whispering, too.

"Want to make a deal," Harve said.

Dingus went to his knees. "What kinder deal?"

"Let me and Betsy go. I'll make it worth your time."

Dingus rose like a jack-in-the-box. "Oh, no, y' don't," he said, "not me, you don't."

"Aw, come on, Dingus—" he stopped speaking, because Dingus had disappeared.

"That's that," Harve muttered, but he didn't relax.

With the fire out, the night cleared and stars twinkled in a cold sky. A chill wind swept down from the icy heights, bringing a freshness tanged with sage and pine. Harve breathed deeply and he suddenly smelled a new odor, a stench that was powerful, entering his nostrils and bringing him quiveringly alert. *Only one smell like that*: *Indian!*

XIII

MARSHAL BILL PELLEY was a man of many traits, none of which included foolishness. He lay in a cluster of rocks where he'd dove from his horse when the rifle sounded. His horse grazed placidly nearby but Pelley didn't move for ten minutes. Even when he heard horsemen leave, the sound dying out, he waited. One man might have been left behind to finish the job.

He was mad as a fresh-cut steer but it didn't show. He made a virtue of patience and while he waited he tried to put the puzzle together. Harve had shouted the warning and this added to the confusion of thoughts. He picked over his experience, trying to find something that matched his present knowledge and there was nothing. He grunted, stuck his hat on the end of his pistol and poked it up over the rocks and waited.

Nothing happened.

Feeling a mite apprehensive, he stood up, clapping his hat on but holding his pistol ready for quick shooting. Walking steadily up the shallow draw, he stepped in between two rocks and stood there while he looked the surroundings over carefully. He began a careful prowl, not missing a foot of ground. Five horses. Four men and the girl. Blood spots by a boulder. He nodded grimly. When Harve shouted a warning someone had clouted him.

Pelley looked off into the distance, sheathing his gun. *Who*, he wondered, *had Harve met here?* He shook his head. It was all a complete mystery and he'd never find the answer standing here.

Got to stop that boy, he thought moodily, as he walked back to his horse. He'd never had a son of his own, in fact had never even considered a family. But if he did have, he'd want him to be like Harve. The kid had the makings of a good man. Conversely, if he didn't get hazed back on the right track, he could become a hell-raising bad one.

Can't let that happen, Pelley thought.

"Me Red Eagle!" The whispered sound came out of the darkness and the yell died in Harve's throat. The pitiful band at Pipestem Springs flashed in his blank mind as the covering came off him.

He had a moment of thankfulness that he'd tried his best to help the Indians as he had, shivering as the knife blade touched his wrist. He felt the pressure of the rawhide relax as the razor-edge knife sliced through the strands. He rolled over and placed his hand close to Betsy's mouth, ready to clamp down if she cried out.

He shook her gently.

He felt her body go rigid, then she relaxed as she recognized him.

"Don't make any racket," he whispered. "We got help. I'll have you loose in a minute." He searched and found his pocket knife and opened the big blade. He cut the ropes that held her.

"Come!" Red Eagle whispered.

Harve shoved Betsy out ahead of him and followed, holding their bedding, something like panic gripping him. The moon came out as Red Eagle led them to the horses. The Indian stood by while Harve tightened the cinches on the black and his roan. He secured the bedrolls and helped Betsy up. Then he mounted.

"Come!" Red whispered again.

"Aiiee, take their horses," Harve said.

Red Eagle drew himself up. "I come back for them," he said, "now, come."

They followed Red Eagle as he made a wide circle, heading down the creek. In less than an hour, the barking dogs picked them up and followed them into the dark and silent camp.

In front of Red Eagle's wickiup, Red Eagle and Harve faced one another.

"You brought much good medicine," Red Eagle said. "My braves killed an elk after your passage. We now have meat in our lodges. We have meat drying on the racks. Our children will not go hungry when the snow falls."

"That's all real nice, Red Eagle," Harve said. "But we gotta get moving before Carney finds out we're gone."

"You stay here," Red Eagle said. "The three men will not find you."

"Can't do that," Harve said. "There'll be others looking for me, too. I don't want you to get tangled up in this mess." He looked around at Betsy. Her horse was standing there and she was nowhere around.

The panic returned. "Where'd the girl go?" he asked in a strangled voice.

Betsy's voice came from the lodge. "I'm here," she said. "I'll be out in a moment, Harve."

He wanted to warn her that the lodge might be infected with lice but he didn't want to offend Red Eagle. He looked at the Indian.

"I don't rightly know just where I am," he said.

Red Eagle pointed across the ridge. "Pipestem Springs there," he said. Half-turning, he pointed again. "Town there."

"We don't want to go to either place," Harve muttered. He offered Red Eagle his hand. "Thanks, mister. You done a lot tonight and I won't forget it."

An Indian girl came out of the lodge. Harve stared. It wasn't an Indian at all but Betsy in buckskin.

"I traded with the Indian," she said shyly. "That dress wasn't exactly a convenience while riding."

"Let's get to gettin'," Harve said gruffly.

As he led out, he wondered where to go, what to do.

It was intensely dark in the canyon and when Harve looked up, the rim of the mountains seemed high above him. The narrow strip of sky was velvet cloth in which the stars sparkled.

It was useless to try to pick a way. He let the horse have a loose rein and looked back from time to time to make sure he didn't lose Betsy. The stream began making noises and he knew it was narrowing and becoming swifter. He could only let the horse drift and hope he wouldn't come on anyone searching for him. There was no doubt in his mind that searching parties would be out.

The walls of the canyon narrowed and grew steeper and the stream dwindled to a trickle; then the land fell away on either side to a broad, flat mesa, and the starshine touched them. Harve stopped to let the winded horses breathe.

"I'm tired," Betsy said as he helped her to the ground. The night was colder than ever and their teeth chattered. Harve and Betsy stood close between the horses, absorbing their own and the animal's heat.

"Guess we'll go on 'til we find a wind break, then make camp." he said by way of comfort.

"What'll we do, Harvey?"

He laughed to cover his lack of an answer. "Guess we'll make out," he said.

She leaned against him. "We're just a couple of children," she whispered, then repeated: "Two children, Harvey."

He stiffened. "Don't fret," he said sharply. "And don't say that. Not like that."

"All right, Harvey," she said softly.

But he knew what she meant. He had a kind of helpless feeling, all the deeper because he couldn't seem to understand what he was doing out there on a lonely mesa with a girl, and with men searching for them—for him at least.

"I didn't mean to shut you off," he said after a long silence. "It's just maybe you're right. Except I never was a kid and can't figure out how it'd feel."

She cried, "Oh, Harvey," and put her head on his chest.

"I think the horses are rested enough," he said gruffly, moving away from her. "Guess we better get moving."

"Where are we, Harvey?"

He shook his head. "Danged if I know. Kind of mixed up in the dark." He helped her to mount and stepped up into his own saddle.

Two hours of steady riding put them across the mesa. As they reached the far rim the sky brightened with the coming of dawn. It was downhill now and as the light grew stronger, Harve could see familiar terrain that brought a thump to his chest.

They were close to Racker's place.

He guided his horse off into a coulee that branched off and into a clump of trees. He helped Betsy dismount and had her wrap herself in a bedroll while he unsaddled and staked out the horses. When he finished this chore he found she had fallen asleep. He gathered firewood and soon had a small fire going. He was too tired to fix anything to eat so he wrapped himself in the other bedroll beside the fire and immediately went to sleep.

Harve awakened to the distant thunder of horses. He flung off the bedroll and ran to the edge of the timber and looked down into the valley. A band of horsemen rode at right angles to where he stood holding the buckbrush branch.

It was a posse, he knew, by the way they spread out and by the rifles they carried across their saddles and the way their heads bobbed watchfully. He sank to the ground on his knees, watching them as they rode out of sight.

He twisted at the sound behind him. Betsy stood looking at him questioningly.

"A bunch just went down the valley," he said, rising to his feet. "Feel like a bit of grub?"

She nodded. "I'm hungry and that's a fact."

He built up the fire, using only dry wood so it wouldn't make smoke. He felt better after the quick, rough meal he put together. He rolled a smoke and lay back on his bedroll.

"What're we going to do, Harvey?"

He looked moodily at the dying fire. "We're close to Racker's place. I'm worried about the old man. When it gets dark I'll ride down and see he's all right."

"Aren't you afraid they'll be watching? They might capture you."

He nodded. "That's why I'll wait 'til dark. Then I can skin in and out easy as eating pie. I know where I am, now."

"I hope you do, Harvey," she said in a soft voice. "I sure do hope you do."

When Dingus called out in alarm at daybreak, Carney came out of his soogan holding his .45 out in front, waving it back and forth. It took him two minutes to find out that Harve and Betsy had disappeared during the night.

"Now, look here, Wes, I didn't stand no watch, we all us slept . . ."

Carney struck him with the pistol barrel, laying it across his cheek and leaving a red gash. Dingus reeled back into Squint, holding his hand to his cheek, blood seeped through his fingers; he wished he had let the kid go. "All right, build up the fire and we'll git somethin' and take out after 'em."

Carney swore until his throat ached as he and his two men huddled around the fire, gulping coffee, staring at one another like strange dogs meeting at the town pump.

Wes snarled wolfishly, "Hurry, damn you both, and let's see if'n we kin track 'em."

"I already seed two sets o' tracks," Squint offered. "Two hosses went one way and three t'other."

"Somebuddy must a cut 'em loose." Carney made a growling sound as he threw the dregs from his cup into the fire. "Shake it."

"We gonna walk?" Squint asked.

Carney glared at him like a wild man. "Naw, we gotta coupla elephants tied up over there and we gonna ride 'em. . . ." He snorted and Squint, with a scared look at

Carney, hurriedly took the trail. Carney and Dingus followed.

Squint was a fair tracker. He went right along as the trail of the two horses circled back toward the creek.

Even so it was more than two hours later that the three outlaws smelled the smoke of the camp. They watched from a distance, hidden by brush and Carney growled, "That damn bunch of reds . . ."

"I don't see our hosses," Dingus said.

"We didn't foller our hosses" Carney contemptuously. "We wuz follerin' the kids."

Carney checked his rifle and pistol. The others hastily followed suit. In a half a minute they made sure their arms were fully loaded.

"We'll get close as we kin," Carney said with a wolfish scowl, "an' the minute they spot us we start shootin'."

They got within fifty feet of the brush huts before a mongrel ran at them with back hair raised and teeth bared. Carney shot the dog and the wickiups erupted. The three of them emptied their pistols and then used their rifles as the Indians ran, trying to escape.

Later, the three walked from hut to hut but they found no living creature.

"Now, let's find them hosses," Carney said.

XIV

HARVE TIED HIS horse in the willows down by the creek below the dark and silent cluster of buildings that was the Double H. He removed his spurs and put them in his saddle bags. The moon was not yet out and the night was dark but not dark enough to obscure the square bulk of Racker's house, Harve's own lean-to and the big old log barn.

Uneasy in his mind, he hesitated in working toward the lean-to he had lived in since his fourteenth birthday, or thereabouts. A brooding sense of danger seemed in the very air he breathed. He had to remind himself that it was only a return of his old childhood fears. The one time Harve remembered Racker laughing fit to kill was at Harve's small-boy fear of wall shadows at night.

The unearthly quiet was upsetting. He had to recall that Racker's place had never been noisy. Not many people come by, even in this hospitable country. Racker had a mean disposition that was forbidding. He exploded if a door happened to bang shut in a stiff wind. *That's it,* he thought with some relief, *no wind tonight.* There was a lull in the wind's incessant rush over the land. That, and the lack of horses in the corral. Racker had probably turned out the few remaining ones after he cut out the bunch to take to town. *Good Lordy,* he thought, *seems like ancient history.* He fervently hoped the old man was all right.

He reached the shelter of the barn without incident and followed the wall to the front. Crouching, he went across the open space to the lean-to. He stopped at the door, his hand on the peg, hearing a deep snore from within.

He had a deepdown lost feeling, listening to the far off lonesome bark of a coyote while the sound of sleep reached him. His very own shack. He'd built it himself. And Racker had let someone take it over. He sucked his breath deep, to try to ease the pain somwhere inside him. *After all,* he thought dully, *nobody's to blame but me. I went off and left him, spent his money gambling and drinking. What right have I got to feel lost just because he got somebody else?*

Shrugging, he turned away from the door and headed directly for the house. He owed it to himself to tell Racker what had happened. He'd stay on and work it off if Racker wanted it that way and the law let him. If it couldn't be worked out, he'd head out somewhere and earn the money and send it to the old man. That way he'd be free of that part of it.

Harve was so familiar with his surroundings that he walked up on the porch, entered the unlocked front door and went straight to the center table that held the lamp. He got a match out of his hatband and scratched it aflame and turned.

Racker had fallen asleep in his chair. The quilt was drooped across his thin legs and his old head leaned on one shoulder; his mouth sagged open, revealing a few snags of yellow teeth in dark red gums. *His color looks better,* Harve thought, as the old man stirred, raised his head, blinking.

"Howdy, Mr. Racker," Harve said.

Racker stiffened, blinking at Harve and his eyes widened in sudden fear as he raised his two hands in a protective gesture.

"I was jus' savin' it fer you, boy," he whined. "I didn't mean t' keep anythin' myself. It was all fer you, just like I promised Hack. . . ." His voice trailed off and then he threw his head back and screamed: "He's here! He's here! Help! Help!" At the same time, he tumbled off the quilt and Harve dropped the match. As the room went dark a gun roared from Racker's direction. He felt the tug of the bullet on his sleeve and dropped to the floor to scramble away from the window. Racker fired two more shots that screamed off the stone fireplace.

Harve looked across the room and was amazed to see a movement as Racker headed for the door. It opened briefly and closed. "Come on, come on!" Racker yelled from the front. "I got him trapped in here!"

Harve heard the pounding of boots as men came from wherever they'd been. He heard their shouted questions and Racker's answer.

"Snuck in on me he did, and tried t' gun me down! He can't get away! A couple you boys light out and find his horse. It'll be around som-ers!"

Racker don't sound much like a sick man, Harve thought. *Must have got some better, in a hurry.* Outside, guns flamed and lead plunked through walls. At least two men had joined Racker in front. Others were surrounding the old house which wasn't built to keep bullets out. He ran to the fireplace and crouched inside, protected on three sides by the stone. The firing increased, lead whispering through the paper-thin walls kept him pinned down.

He had to get out. He'd been a fool to try and see the old man. *Must be dingy,* he thought, *talking crazy like he did.*

Harve thought about taking a running plunge through the window but they'd all turn their guns on him and nail him for sure. If only he could get outside the darkness would help shield him. It'd take them some time to find his horse. He had to get to the roan before they did or he'd be afoot. That would hamper him something terrible. But it seemed that the only way was to shoot himself out of this trap and trust to luck. He spun the cylinder of his pistol, took a cartridge out of a belt loop and held open the loading gate while he located the empty chamber he usually carried under the hammer. He slid the brass in and let the loading gate click shut.

The firing outside slacked off. *Now,* he thought, *while they're reloading.* He came out of the fireplace and ran for the door when a windowpane crashed and a blazing pine knot landed in the center of the room, flaring up as it skidded along the floor. He whirled and scooted back into the fireplace as the guns set up a clamor, the bullets whanging off into space as they caromed from the stone fireplace.

"Come out with your hands up!" a strident voice called.

Wonder who that is, Harve thought, not answering.

"Come out, damn you, or we'll roast you!"

Harve glanced toward the wall where the pine knot blazed furiously, ignited the tinder dry wall boards. The circle of light grew and shadows danced on the ceiling. In another moment, the entire wall was ablaze and the room was filled with smoke. The flames licked toward the ceiling and the pine wood crackled furiously as the fire ate its way toward him with lightning speed.

He wiped his face on his arm, the one that held the pistol. If he ran out shooting they'd cut him down. If he stayed here he'd roast.

The smoke came into the fireplace and was drawn up the chimney. Harve looked upward, hope flaming as high as the fire itself. The twinkle of stars reached him. He stood up, mindless of the soot-blackened stone.

"Come out while you still got a chance!" The voice raised higher: "Spread out boys, he's liable to come out shootin'!"

Harve got a lungful of smoke, his eyes watering, coughing behind a clenched fist. Shoving his pistol in his holster, he grabbed the projections of the stone and hoisted himself up, caught a foothold, and went up, gaining a foot or two at a time. On up, he scrambled in a cloud of dense smoke that seemed to grow thicker as he neared the top. Eyes smarting, gasping for breath, he used the last of his strength to shove himself above the rim of the chimney, feeling the first breath of fresh air clearing his lungs and head.

The far side of the house lighted with the blaze. A group of men stood there, waiting with drawn guns. He slipped over the edge of the chimney and went down the dark side, hoping the house would not be entirely surrounded.

His feet touched the ground and he went to his belly and wiggled away into the outer darkness. Far out away from the house, he stood up and ran for the willows and untied his horse. Looking at the house as he mounted, he saw the flames break through the roof, lighting up the entire area. He rode the horse back toward the camp, where he'd left Betsy.

No use trying to talk to a crazy man, he thought, with a heavy heart. *Why had Racker told those men that I tried to gun him down?* He shook his head in a fresh wave of despair. He'd never get out of this now, no matter how hard he tried. He showed his face and Racker'd have that bunch of gunhawks waiting for him.

He felt the horse shiver under him as a rifle blasted. He

only had time to disengage his feet from the stirrups as the roan fell heavily.

"Got 'im!" someone shouted and footsteps pounded toward him.

XV

It was a slow day in Jemez Springs. The town was gathering itself for payday at the mine and sawmill, a once a month occurrence that tried the souls of townsmen but filled their pockets.

A gathering of men, including Wendel Morrow, waited the arrival of the stage, which was making dust up the road.

"Sure in a hurry," someone remarked, and a tremor of expectation ran through the group, like wind moves the prairie grass.

The horses were covered with lather as the driver hauled them to a stop before the clapboard shanty fronting the wagon yard.

"What's the trouble, Hank?" the agent called as Hank wrapped the reins around the brake handle.

"Holdup," Hank said briefly.

All eyes were on the canvas-wrapped bundle behind the driver and guard.

"You didn't lose the payroll?" the mine super called and Hank shook his head.

Wendel Morrow saw all the passengers off as the talk buzzed. When the last one stepped down, he wondered why Betsy, the niece he'd never met, wasn't on the stage. Morrow was a man of fifty-odd rough-lived years, with a pointed gray beard and a pair of eyebrows like two furry worms perched above cold gray eyes. He was dressed in elegant clothing, white ruffled shirt under swallow-tailed coat and soft expensive boots.

"Didn't you bring a girl?" he asked the driver.

93

The gaunt man swung down from the driver's seat. "Yeah. Like I said, we had trouble."

The crowd grew larger and gathered closer, completely surrounding the stage.

"Well," Morrow said patiently.

"Seems two holdup men had a difference," the driver related. "They shot it out an' t'other one took off cross country."

"What about the girl?" Morrow's voice sharpened.

"Gettin' to that. She went after him."

A murmur ran through the crowd like wind in the pine trees.

"Of her own free will?" Morrow asked.

"Yep. Tried to call her back. She wouldn't stop, kept a-goin." He looked at the guard. "Come on, let's get this strongbox off 'fore somebuddy else tries for it."

"Where'd it happen?" Morrow asked in a steely voice.

"On first grade comin' up Nine Mile Canyon," the driver said, as he and the guard muscled the strongbox to the ground where the station agent and mine super took it over.

Morrow climbed to the top step of the stage station. "Any of you men want to ride down there, be ready in fifteen minutes," he called. "I'll appreciate any and all help. Bring your own ammunition and trail grub."

Without waiting for a commitment, he hurried down the street to an ornate house on the edge of town. A tall girl with high-piled blonde hair met him at the door.

"Where is she?" the tall girl, Alice Taynor, wanted to know.

He grimaced in disgust. "Ran off with some stickup artist," he said, brushing past the woman. There were three other girls in the room, two of them playing concentration and the other buffing her fingernails. They looked at Morrow without emotion.

He went on through the room and when he emerged ten minutes later he wore clothing more suitable for riding in rough country. A gun belt was strapped around his waist and he carried a rifle in the crook of his arm.

"Didn't think I'd ever put this on again," he said, touching the butt of his pistol.

"You really didn't think you'd put it away for good?" Alice asked.

He nodded his head. "When I quit bounty huntin' that was it. This is different."

She followed him outside and watched as he headed toward the corner of the house and on to the barn. She called, "You'll be back before the payday crowd gets here?"

He stopped before he turned the corner. "I'll be back when I find the girl." Then he walked on.

The woman shrugged. It was his worry. She just worked there.

In five minutes, Morrow reined his horse up before the clapboard shack in front of the wagon yard. Three riders waited for him. He knew them for drifters but he didn't care. That they were looking for excitement made little difference to him. He'd used men like these before.

He looked at each man in turn. They were uneasy under his stare. He appeared a different man than the fancy dude who'd asked them to help him find a girl. His eyes showed the steel more plainly in rough range clothes.

"All right," he said at last. "I'd hoped for a few more than three. Not that it matters. Let's go."

The dark form of a man leaped toward Harve, holding a rifle across his body with both hands. He stopped abruptly and raised the rifle as Harve sidestepped and swung the pistol in his hand. He caught the man full in the face with the frame of the gun, dropping him. The other man crashed through the brush and Harve's action was mechanical. He simply thumbed back the hammer of his Colt and let it fall. There was a stab of flame and a roar and the other man catapulted backward.

For a moment Harve stood there peering through the smoke, smelling the sharp odor of gunpowder, sheer panic gripping him. In the space of two days he'd gunned down

95

two men. How many more would he have to shoot in fighting for his life?

The man on the ground he'd slugged groaned and set him in motion. He heard shouts and calls in the distance toward Racker's as he scrambled up and away. A sob escaped him as he thought of his horse back there on the ground. He'd raised the roan from a colt, feeding with a bottle after the mare that foaled it fell prey to a mountain lion.

He ran through the night and gradually the sounds died away. He rested, drawing deep painful breaths while a sharp pain sliced his side. He waited until his breathing quieted and then walked on as a false dawn grayed the eastern sky.

There was no trail and he struggled up the rocky slope with the sky brightening all the time. By the time he reached the head of the draw it was full daylight. He heard the sound of a horse and moved aside into the brush, drawing his pistol as he did so. He replaced the gun when he saw Betsy, riding the black, heading toward him. He stepped out and raised his hand in greeting.

Her face showed glad surprise as she slipped from the saddle and ran to him. He held her loosely while he listened to her outpouring of worry and fear.

"I heard shooting. I was scared before that but afterward I thought I'd die. I had to do something. I thought maybe you might need me."

He saw the color return to her face and he thought she was beautiful. "I lost my horse," he said.

"We still have one left." She stepped away from him, blushing. "I left everything back where we camped."

"We'd better pick it up and move on. They'll be riding up that draw in no time."

"Harvey?"

He looked at her.

"Please don't leave me alone again."

"All right. Let's see if this horse will ride double. He might buck a little at first so hang on tight." He stepped up in the saddle and disengaged his left foot from the stirrup and helped her up behind him. He felt her arms encircle his waist and tighten. He kept the black under close rein and urged him out. The horse didn't want to carry double but he moved along, mincing uneasily at first but finally settling down under Harve's soothing voice. Betsy's arms didn't relax for a moment but he didn't mind.

"Don't know why it is," he said, "but I don't feel lonesome no more. For the first time in my life I ain't lonesome."

She didn't answer but her arms tightened around him.

"Did you see Mr. Racker?"

Have nodded. "He sounded like he was out of his head. Kept sayin' something about he didn't mean to do it, didn't mean to keep something from me, or kind of like that. Then he yelled for help and skittered out the door spry as you please." He paused while he ran it through his mind with his forehead wrinkled. "Told the men outside I tried to gun him. All I did was say 'howdy.'"

He felt her shiver.

"Why is the Double H called that, Harvey?"

"I dunno. I asked Racker once and he blessed me out good, said it wasn't any o' my business. Then a couple days later he said when he got the spread he was so tickled he yelled, 'hallelujah, hallelujah,' so he just naturally called it the Double H. Why you want to know?"

"I just wondered. Your initials are HH."

"Yeah, it just happened that way, I reckon."

They rode on in silence, then, "Harvey?"

"Yeah?"

"That friend of yours, Price . . . he knew the man who attacked me."

"Wes Carney?"

"Yes, that's the one. I saw him talking to Price in Rowel that day. They were back near the hotel barn, like they didn't want to be seen. Talking real confidential like."

Harve shook his head. "Can't imagine why. But old

Price was a real friendly feller. Always talking to somebody."
He didn't want to talk about Price or think about him either.
He tried to put the man out of his mind and couldn't. It was
a funny thing but he still liked Price and wished with all his
heart things hadn't happened as they had. He shrugged.
*No use crying over something that was gone and couldn't
be helped.*

They reached camp and Harve hurriedly packed camp
gear and bedrolls. Harve was beginning to worry about their
lack of food. They had a limited supply left and he didn't
know where more could be found without great risk. *It'd
be suicide to ride into any sort of settlement,* Harve thought.
Pelley had probably warned the whole territory about him.
Men with guns would be looking for him.

A distant sound tightened his gut until it ached. He
motioned Betsy to be quiet, her wide, frightened eyes somehow softening his own panic.

He catfooted to the edge of the circle of brush and looked
out. He saw nothing, but the sound of approaching riders
grew louder.

As he squatted there in the brush, two horsemen appeared
not more than a hundred feet away and rode slowly from
left to right. He watched them, holding his breath, until
they disappeared from his view.

Betsy spoke from behind his shoulder, whispering. "Who
is it?"

"I dunno. But whoever it is they're probably lookin for
me." He felt buffeted by fate, filled with hopelessness and
helpless as a newborn calf. He didn't tell Betsy but he had a
feeling that he was in a circle that was closing in on him
by the minute.

XVI

THERE HAD BEEN little talk as Harve worked the horse
across rocky ground, through talus and up a wide, shallow
stream to hide their tracks. They came suddenly on a well-

marked camping place, with a half dozen rings of ashes marking campfires, and a clear spring bubbling from around the roots of a gnarled old oak.

Harve sat his horse looking at the notice that had been nailed to the tree. Riding high on the bedrolls, Betsy gasped and put her hands on his shoulders.

The notice written in pencil in big block letters simply said:

NOTICE TO HARVEY HOLLEY: NO REASON TO KEEP RUNNING AND MAYBE GET SHOT. YOU ARE NOT AN OUTLAW BUT WILL BE IF YOU KEEP ON. BILL PELLEY, MARSHAL.

"It's a trick," Harve said. He looked all around, suddenly cautious again. "Just a mean rotten trick."

"Maybe it's not," Betsy said doubtfully.

"Well, I'm not taking any chances," Harve said stubbornly and put the black in motion.

A half hour later, he stopped at the entrance to a small canyon. To the south, he could see a circle of buzzards wheeling almost without wing motion against the breaks of blue. For some reason the sight of the carrion eaters made him shiver. He turned the horse into the canyon. When the walls closed in, he left the canyon and headed the willing black toward the leafy draw. Deep in the buckbrush, screened by high walled slopes and plenty of cover, he threw a leg over the horn and slid to the ground.

"We'll be all right here for a spell," he said and reached up to help Betsy to the ground. "Don't like to use that horse too much."

They spent the rest of the day in the brush, listening to the wild sounds of the rising wind, watching the clouds build up to the west. Overhead, the quick scudding lower clouds drifted past, thickening.

"Gonna rain," he said and offered her a piece of the jerky that Red Eagle had given them. He watched the movements of her soft jawline as she chewed the leathery strip and had a funny unfamiliar feeling deep inside him. Kind of like he wanted to protect her from anything bad happening. The black switched its tail and stopped grazing to raise its head, ears pointed forward.

Harve came to his feet in one easy move, jerking out his pistol and motioning the girl to keep quiet. He looked in the direction the horse was looking and could see nothing at all. He put a finger to his lips and catfooted through the brush. The darting coyote ran ahead of him and Harve relaxed, chuckling with relief, and put his pistol away. He turned and walked slowly back to where Betsy waited.

"What was it?" she asked, seeing the relief in his face.

"Just a coyote snooping around." He hoped she wouldn't think he was too scary. He went to the black and began inspecting its hoof. He used the butt of his knife to tighten a nail on the left fore-hoof. He didn't stop until he had looked at all four hoofs. He let the last drop to the ground, closed the knife and dropped it into his pocket.

"What're we going to do?"

"Don't keep asking," he said shortly.

"You don't know, that's why you snap at me."

"I didn't snap at you. I just wish you'd quit pecking at me. I didn't ask you to come." A resolve had suddenly formed in his mind. Almost as if a solution had been given him. She had no business out in the brush with him. She ought to be with her uncle, no matter how mean and lowdown he might be. She couldn't be worse off anywhere than here with him.

"I'm not pecking," she said with some spirit. "I just—"

"Well, don't," he forced himself to bark. "Just about one more word and I'll pack you off to Jemez Springs where you belong."

She was silent, not looking at him, her fingers busy with the buckskin fringe on the skirt that Red Eagle's squaw had traded her.

He gave her a guarded look, her bowed head giving him a twinge in his guts.

"Thinks that's what I ought t' do anyway," he muttered, pulling out his tobacco sack. It didn't have enough tobacco left for even one thin quirly. He tossed the sack away with a sound of disgust.

Betsy put her face in her hands and Harve swallowed hard, mentally swore and scrubbed his knuckles against his jaw.

Contriteness moved him toward her, destroying his resolve to send her on to Jemez Springs one way or another. Somewhere in the distance a horse struck a rock with an iron shoe. Harve halted in midstride and Betsy raised startled eyes to him.

Tiny bumps formed on Harve's arm. He felt panic grab at him, and he had to force himself to keep from blind, unreasoning flight. He thought, with a sudden yearning which squeezed his heart, of the old days before things became so complicated. He recalled the peace that he'd scoffed at while he had it. Now, if only he were back in that time and place. . . .

The horses were nearer now. A man's voice spoke in a strangely familiar way. Harve's heart convulsed and then raced. It was a voice he'd heard the night before at Racker's.

"I know he come this way," the man was saying. "You ain't the only tracker, Spade."

"Yeah, but I say he went out t'other side, Crick."

Crick Justan and Spade Cooley! A couple of mean, no-good gunhawks. Harve had heard a lot of wild tales about their doings.

Harve was at the black's head in two steps, placing his hand over the velvet muzzle, ready to squeeze off a sound at the slightest belly swell. The black stood very still as though aware he should not make a sound.

The noise of the horses stopped. The horsemen had halted a dozen feet, beyond a thick cluster of brush. Saddle leather creaked and Harve heard the soft chime of a spur. He turned his head as Betsy stood beside him. He whispered:

"They'll go in a minute. Keep quiet."

Beads of sweat glistened on her upper lip. She looked pale and frightened. He felt a strange yearning twist his heart and he wanted to put his arm protectively around her. He put away that vagrant thought, suddenly stiffening.

"Here, what . . . hey, Crick . . ." A thud of hoofs and brush cracked. Without trying to salvage anything, Harve boosted Betsy atop the horse and leaped up behind her. Guns roared and a bullet whined off a tree limb. His spurless heels drummed the black's ribs as the horse bolted. He caught a glimpse of a racing horseman ahead. He felt Betsy flinch as another shot sounded. He reined sharp right and let the frightened black have its lead.

"After 'em," Crick bawled, "don't let 'im get away."

They rode hard for a quarter-mile before Harve slowed the sweating horse. Betsy was crumpled against him. His left arm was encircling her and he raised it, seeing the blood on his arm. He hastily clasped her to him to keep her from falling.

She'd been hit.

He slid off and let her fall into his arms. He stood there holding her, feeling a sick helplessness engulf him. Her head fell limply across his arm and her eyes were closed. He couldn't tell if she was breathing or not.

He had the reins looped around his arm. The black, smelling the blood, was dancing excitedly. Harve spoke soothingly to the horse and the act of gentling the animal had a similar effect on him. He knelt, laying Betsy gently on the ground. The blood was flowing freely down her neck and onto the buckskin; the sight of it scared him even more. He raised the thick mass of black hair. The bullet, maybe a ricochet, from the looks of the ragged wound, had struck just above the ear and coursed around the curve of her head. She lay quiet as death but she still breathed.

Oh, Lordy, he thought, *whatever am I gonna do now?*

He listened but couldn't hear any sound that indicated pursuit. He couldn't be sure, though. *Good gravy,* he thought, *they must have the whole county out looking for me. This,* he reasoned, *is it.*

He tried to remember the lay of the land. Off to the southeast was the general direction of Racker's place. He couldn't go there. Nearest neighbor to Racker was Jess Sykes' little baling wire outfit, about fifteen miles across the ridge. That would place Sykes' place nearest to him. He could get help there. Sykes rarely left the ranch except to buy supplies a couple of times a year. Chances were good Sykes didn't even know about the big commotion going on.

He listened again and could hear nothing. That sharp, right angle change of direction might have thrown them off. But if they were any good at tracking, and he supposed they were as they'd followed him through some difficult country, it wouldn't take long to pick up the trail.

Harve lifted Betsy on the black and held her, while he led the horse to a shallow cutbank. There, he eased on the sleek back behind Betsy, cradling her body against his own. He turned the black and headed in the direction of Sykes' place, keeping the horse in a fast walk.

He had to stop and hide once. He put the black into a clump of thick-growing cedar that tore at his face, and waited, holding Betsy with one hand, his pistol with the other. The noise soon receded and he went on as a sliver of moon poked from behind a cloud, dimly lighting the way. On top of the mountain, the valley below was dark. Harve reasoned, *that means nothing. Sykes and his clan went to bed with the chickens.*

The black picked its slow and careful way down the mountain. It was past midnight when Harve, dogtired, reined up in front of the log house that sheltered the Sykes family. He slid to the ground and got Betsy off the horse, still unconscious. She had not stirred since being hit and his worry deepened. She felt slack, her body limp in his arms.

"Hallooooo, the house!" he yelled.

He heard a calf bawl somewhere off in the darkness but no sound inside the cabin. He walked to the door and kicked it. The sound was loud but brought no response. He shoved at the door—the bar wasn't in place and the door opened. It was more dark inside than out. He placed Betsy on the floor and searched his hatband for a match and scratched it into flame, holding it over his head. There was a candle on a table. He cupped his hand around the flame and walked slowly so as not to jostle it out, and lighted the stub of wax.

The one large room held a combination cooking and heating stove, a table, and four chairs. There was a ladder in one corner leading to the attic. The house seemed deserted, as though everything movable had been hurriedly taken away.

There was a cold flapjack on the stove and he ate it as he built a fire. When the fire was going good he searched around and found a battered old pail. He went outside and stood in the dark until his vision altered so he could see the outline of the well near the house. He walked through the night, drew a bucket of water, filled the pail and returned to the house with it. He found a tin cup in the cupboard, filled it with water and carried it to Betsy. He raised her and let the water trickle into the mouth. Her throat worked and part of the water spilled on her buckskin jacket.

Then Harve began a methodical search of the cabin, looking for medicine. In the cupboard, he found a bottle of Dr. Putney's cough syrup, a small squat bottle of Old Lavender Smelling Salts and a pint bottle of turpentine. With the water and turpentine, he began cleansing the wound. Her face was hot and he suspected she had fever.

She sighed as he cleaned the wound but didn't regain consciousness. She moved uneasily as he let turpentine dribble on the jagged cut.

He was tense with concern and apprehension. *Got to get her to a doctor,* he thought, *one way or another.* Nearest town was Rowel and he was too well-known there. *But no matter,* he told himself, *I got to get help for her.*

He walked restlessly up and down the cabin and then wheeled and went outside. The wind was rising and a few drops of rain fell on his face. Morning light was a long time coming and he was impatient for it. He found wood and returned to the cabin.

When the sky grayed enough to give him some light he went outside again, feeling depressed. There was nothing in the barn except a few scraps of harness hanging on one dusty wall. There was a rickety buckboard against the back of the house. He pulled it out, its wheels creaking dryly. It was a single horse rig and all he needed was a horse to pull it.

He looked at the black grazing on the sparse grass nearby, shaking his head at the thought of trying to make a harness horse out the spirited animal.

He searched every corner of the barn again but couldn't find the collar or hames for which he looked. He did discover an old pair of cracked breeching, a breast strap with the traces gone. Further searching turned up hobbles and a set of driving reins. He spliced the reins to make traces and took his finds to the horse.

The black, as he expected, fought the harness. Harve gradually quieted him and led him to the buckboard. It took ten minutes of hard work to get the black between the shafts. Finally, he had the horse harnessed and hitched. He tied the animal to the corner of the house and went inside the cabin.

He needed something to wrap Betsy in. Climbing the ladder he looked into the attic. There was a ragged blanket on a straw mattress. He grabbed it up and started down the ladder. Something hanging on the wall caught his eye. It looked like a scalp hanging from a nail on the wall. He took it down and inspected it curiously.

It was a long switch of human hair, the kind women used to appear to have much more hair than they naturally have.

He'd heard about these things but this was the first one he'd seen and it gave him an idea.

He removed his hat, draped the thing, women called a "rat," around his chin and tied the two ends on top and replaced his hat. *It feels like a beard,* he thought, as he fingered it. His upper lip was smooth except for soft down but then lots of men wore beards without mustache. In a pinch it might serve to hide his identity.

He lifted Betsy and carried her out of the cabin to the buckboard. He placed her on the spring planks, tucked the blanket around her and climbed down, talking soothingly to the trembling black. He untied the horse and worked back to the buckboard, holding the reins taut as he made it to the seat.

The black immediately went into a gallop. Harve was afraid the ancient vehicle would fly to pieces. He held in the reins, talking in a soft voice; and, after a quarter-hour of gentling, the black decided to resign himself to the indignity of pulling a buckboard.

A feeling of excitement and purpose began to come over him. It was hard to believe that anyone would be taken in by his disguise but it might give him a chance to get in and get out of town. He hoped Marshal Pelley wouldn't be around. He'd be a hard one to fool.

He came on to the main road and still hadn't met anyone. Afternoon was waning when he smelled the woodsmoke of Rowel. As he passed a cabin on the road, the aroma of coffee made his belly churn.

The black walked across the bridge and Harve entered town in late afternoon. It was during the supper hour and not many people were about. He drove to the Central corral and got down.

He had a prickly feeling that he was being watched. Looking toward the back door of the hotel, he saw someone in the shadows. His heart convulsed and raced like a wild horse as the dark figure stepped out of the shadows to come toward him.

XVII

By RELENTLESS TRACKING, Crick Justan and Spade Cooley reached the Sykes place just an hour after Harve and Betsy left in the buckboard.

Justan put his hand on the stove. "Still warm," he said, as Cooley entered the cabin.

"Nothin' in the barn," Cooley said. "Some buggy tracks right outside the door."

"Musta been somebuddy else," Justan said. "Sykes didn't have no buggy."

"Buckboard, then. Hit'd been settin' fur a long spell back o' th' house. Wheels sunk in soft dirt and grass growed up around 'em."

"An ol' buckboard," Justan mused. "I 'member seein' hit. Sykes had a spring waggin he used t' haul in." He walked up and down the cabin, stopping at the clutter in the middle of the room, battered pail, tin cup and bottles. He squatted, picked up the turpentine and sniffed it. "Somebuddy got hurt," he said in a soft and pleased voice.

"I tol' you I hit 'im," Cooley said excitedly.

"Naw. You hit that gal," Justan corrected, rising, his eyes gleaming. "He's haulin' that gal inter town, that's what he's doin'."

"He wouldn't go t' town," Cooley grunted. "Ever damn body in the county's lookin' fur—" He broke off and dashed to the window at the sound of horses.

Justan ran to the other window, drawing his pistol. Three men dismounted a respectable distance away and stood there looking at the cabin.

"Who the hell you reckon that is?" Cooley wondered.

"I dunno," Justan said, "but I aim t' find out." He slid his pistol in his side pocket but kept his fingers curled around the butt. Walking to the door, he jerked it open and stepped outside.

The three men a hundred feet away drifted apart almost imperceptibly.

"Howdy, stranger," Justan called cheerfully, smiling. "Crick Justan here and my pard, Spade Cooley. We part o' a posse."

"Who you lookin' fur?" the red-headed man called.

"Kid name Harve Holley, killed a feller and kidnapped a girl of'n the Rowel stage."

The three men looked at one another. The red-headed man turned back to Justan. "I'm Wes Carney and these two fellars are Dingus McBride and Squint Cullers. We lookin' for the same kid, Crick."

"Well, whatta y' know! Come on in th' house, Wes."

The three men consulted in low voices and then walked forward leading their horses, while Crick Justan surreptitiously holstered his pistol, motioned to Cooley and the two walked out to meet the new arrivals.

The air cleared at once as the five men inspected one another. In each other they recognized a fellow shadow rider. Each of them felt the mantle of comradeship fall into place.

"We ain't got much grub," Crick said, "an' I see you all are ridin' light."

"The kid's been here?" Wes Carney asked, his eyes slitted.

"Yeah, stove still warm. He's headin' fer Rowel."

"Rowel! Why, damn it, he'll get arrested down there. Why'd he go t' Rowel?"

"Figger the gal got hurt," Crick said carelessly. "Figger he took her in t' a doc."

"Well, if'n you don't mind, we'll ride on," Carney said. "Get some grub in town."

"That bein' the case we'll ride along, too," Crick said, adding innocently, "that is, if'n you don't mind."

"Why, shore, come along if y' want," Carney said with equal equanimity.

"Le's quit playin'," Crick said. "We done spent a lot o' time lookin' fur that kid. What you want him about?"

"Why, ain't ever son who kin fork a hoss lookin' fer 'im?"

108

"Yeah, but ever son don't know old man Racker's gonna give us five hundred dollars if we bring him in."

Dingus and Squint tittered and Wes Carney's face mirrored a look of pleasure. "Five hundred? That's chicken feed, Crick." He glanced at Dingus and Squint, hesitated, and then went on: "Old man Racker's got a lot o' gold, maybe fifty thousand dollars. We was gonna use that kid to pry it out o' him. You wanta pitch in with us?"

Crick Justan bellowed with laughter. "Fifty thousand dollars? Old man Racker? Gawd, he don't have fifty thousand cents, Wes. You been hearin' fairy tales." He suddenly sobered as he caught the flinty look in Carney's eyes. He stuck his head forward, staring. "You sure?"

"Yeah, I'm sure," Carney said.

Crick Justan looked at Spade Cooley. "How 'bout it, Spade? You have your druthers what'll it be?"

"Fifty thousand," Spade drawled unhesitatingly. "To hell with ol' man Racker! Five hundred! That ol' buzzard buyin' us off fur that kinder money!"

"Like you said, Wes," Crick said in a kindly voice, "we kin grub up in town."

From a wandering trapper Bill Pelley learned that a bunch of Indians had been massacred on Cow Creek. The buckskin-clad man knew nothing about the circumstances surrounding the killings. Pelley knew the laconic mountain man would not have mentioned it at all if he'd wanted to conceal information from him.

"Sign fresh when I come on it," the old man said. "Not a livin' soul left, braves, squaws, kids, all shot down." He produced a bundle of clothing—women's clothing, including a funny yellow hat. "Found these in one o' th' lodges but no sign o' a white women." He looked at the sky. "Gonna storm and what sign there is'll be wiped out."

He got down on his knees and scraped the ground clean and picked up a stick. "Here's how the camp lay." He traced it out in the dirt as he talked. "Way I read sign, two

109

people, friendly like, led by Injun come first." He looked up at Pelley. "You want t' know all this here, Marshal?"

Pelley nodded. It was out of his jurisdiction, but he was a man dedicated to law and justice. Whatever he learned, he'd pass on to the sheriff in due time. And it might help him now.

"Woman made trade like enough. Her tracks went to lodge in shoes come out in mocassins."

That would be Betsy, Pelley thought, nodding.

"I picked up sign where three men on foot snuck up on 'em. Done the killin' an' rode off on three hosses as had been hid out in a near gully." He tossed the stick down and rose, pointing southeast. "Big fire off over there early mornin'. I could see the flames from Cold Deck Mountain. Still smokin' when day come." He shook his head sadly. "Country's goin' plain t' hell. Reckon that's why I don't go t' town much." He shouldered his pack and trudged off up the creek.

"Thanks for your help," Pelley called, but the mountain man didn't even look back.

Pelley debated on a choice of three actions and he didn't debate long. He could continue the slow, painful work of tracking Harve, who was getting foxier all the time at hiding his trail; he saw little to be gained in investigating the site of the Indian massacre on Cow Creek; a third choice was to ride straight to the scene of the fire—the Double H. He hoped to hell Harve hadn't returned there to start a ruckus.

In time he rode into the Double H ranch. Burt Racker was all alone, sitting in the doorway of the lean-to near the barn, surveying the black square that had been his home.

Pelley dismounted and stretched his aching bones.

The old man looked beaten.

"Glad you're here, Marshal," he said. "I've got a bear by the tail and can't let go."

"Better tell me about it," Pelley said testily, the hard riding he'd done lately honing his temper sharp.

Racker spoke in a monotone, not looking at Pelley.

"It all started a long time ago," he began, "when a man named Hack Holley left his kid here. . . ."

Harve relaxed when he saw the form take shape. It was the woman, Belle, who Price Waldrip had introduced him to. She was holding her skirts so they wouldn't interfere with her fast walk toward him.

She stopped in front of him, looking up at him. "Harvey," she said and her eyes went past him to the buckboard.

He fingered the hair on his chin and then sheepishly jerked it off. "I'm in real trouble, ma'am," he said.

"I'll back you up on that," she said sharply. "You'd better come upstairs . . ."

"I got that girl. There in the buckboard. She's hurt. Bad." He tried to swallow the lump in his throat.

She went past him and he smelled the perfume, remembering the night he'd met her. That seemed like a hundred years ago.

Belle leaned over the buckboard and then straightened, turning. "Take her to my room. I'll find the doctor."

"I don't know where your room is," Harve said.

"Go up the back stairs. First door on the right at the top of the stairway. Get her out of these filthy clothes . . . no, wait, I'll do that when I get back." She stood there with her hands on her hips looking at him with a sad expression, shaking her head. "Go on, get a move on you!"

Harvey said, "Yes'm," and lifted Betsy in his arms. He headed for the hotel's back door. He looked around when he reached the door and found that Belle had disappeared.

Going up the gloomy stairwell he pushed open the first door on the right. It was a fancy place, with a flowered shade on the lamp and a shiny coverlet on the big bed. He laid Betsy on the fancy cover and went to the window to pull the shade.

He turned, surveying the room. There was a big mirror above a dressing table that held all manner of jars, bottles, powder boxes and whatnots. He got a glimpse of himself in the big mirror and stared, hardly recognizing himself. There was dirt and dried blood on his face where he'd been pistol whipped. His shirt was torn and a big gap showed in his pants leg. "You're a total mess," he told himself in the mirror. "A sight in this world."

Footsteps pounded outside and Belle hurried in followed by a little bald-headed man carrying a black bag.

"Doc Spicer," she said briefly.

The little man nodded, removed his coat and tossed it across the foot of the bed. He hauled another chair up beside the bed, sat in it and leaned forward to examine Betsy.

After a moment, he glanced at Harvey.

"How'd it happen?"

"That there's a bullet wound," Harvey said. "She got shot."

"That's plain as day," the doctor said mildly. "I was thinking of why she was shot and all that."

"Well, it's a kinda long story . . ."

"Never mind," the doctor said irritably. "You got to report this to Marshal Pelley." He took a pair of scissors out of his black bag.

Harve flinched at the sight of the scissors and then relaxed as the doctor began trimming the thick black hair from around the wound.

"Pelley's not in town," Belle said. "I'll tell him soon as he gets back."

"After that Racker kid, I suppose."

Harve swallowed, looking at the doctor but the medical man was busy examing Betsy. Belle caught his arm and pulled him out of the room, into the hallway and closed the door.

"She'll be all right," she said comfortingly. "What about you, Harvey, what about you?"

"I got her here, that's the main thing. I haven't planned ahead of that. Get out of town, I suppose."

"You realize you'll be an outlaw if you keep on? Always on the move, afraid to meet an honest man face to face?"

"I'm already that way," he said with resignation. "No

help for that now. I just don't want to be caught . . . locked up."

She shook his arm. "No, it's not too late. Pelley tried to tell you there's no charges against you . . . tried to let you know. He left notes at all the waterholes and camp grounds . . ."

"Just a trick," Harve said.

"No trick. He wanted to stop you before you got in real trouble. Sooner or later you'll cross over, Harvey, and then it'll be too late." Her voice was so emotion-charged he looked sharply at her.

"Why you takin' all this trouble for me?"

She turned away from his stare. "I—I knew your father," she said at last.

"My pa?" he asked wonderingly. He walked to her, touching her arm, then taking it in his hand. "You knew my pa?"

She nodded. "He—he was a good friend."

He asked a question then that'd bothered him most of his life. "Why'd he go off and leave me with Racker?"

"He couldn't help it," she said swiftly. "A man does what he has to do Harvey."

Harvey laughed. "Well, I reckon. And I guess I'll be driftin'. No sense waitin' around here for Pelley to grab me."

"Or all the others," she said.

"What about them others?"

She looked as though she would cry. "Harvey, everybody in the country is after you. Racker offered a reward. That girl's uncle, from Jemez Springs, is a tough nut and has a posse out for you, along with every gun slinger, out-of-work cowhand, and anyone else who can fork a horse. I'm surprised you got the girl here." She swung around and grabbed his shoulders in her two hands and shook him. "Your best bet is to find Bill Pelley and give yourself up."

He pulled away. "I reckon not. I'm beholden to you but

I gotta go now." He stepped away and went down the stairs, walking fast so he wouldn't change his mind.

It was full night outside. Movement in town was like the murmur of water in a canyon creek. Harve stood at the back entrance to the hotel and scanned the area between him and the barn. The black, tied back there, was still hitched to the buckboard. *Poor damn horse,* he thought, and took a deep breath, heading for the horse and rig.

Halfway there he stopped. What had Belle said? *Your best bet is to find Bill Pelley and give yourself up.* He halted again after taking a few steps. That woman up there had known his father. After all these years he had the answer to a mystery and he was taking out like a turpentined dog.

And that stuff about giving himself up. It made sense, if for no other reason that he'd be rid of the awful dread that he'd be caught at any moment. It was a wearing business, this being on the run. He'd had enough of it.

He went on slowly, thinking, *well, I'll take the black out and think on it some more.*

Unhooking the makeshift traces he led the black out from between the shafts and let them fall. He stripped the sorry harness he'd patched up and threw it aside; he rubbed the black down and then tied the animal to a wheel of the buckboard and returned to the hotel.

He had to talk with Belle.

Harve was halfway up the stairs when he heard the horsemen enter the alley leading to the barn. He stopped there in the darkness until the group of men rode past, his guts chilling.

"There's the buckboard," he heard someone—Wes Carney —speak out. "That's Price's black."

XVIII

Harve crouched on the dark stairway, listening to Wes Carney and the others. He clearly identified the voices, wondering how this crew had come together. He didn't have to wonder about their purpose.

"He's likely in Belle's room," Carney said. "Two you boys stake out front an' other two at the back. I'll go up and check."

Harve went up the steps three at a time, came into the dimly lighted hallway just as Belle's door opened. She came out quickly, closing the door behind her.

"They're out there," Harve said, gesturing with his pistol. "Wes Carney an' some more. I don't know how many."

"Get in my room," Belle urged in a whisper. "I'll tell him you're not here."

Harve laughed a little wildly. "He won't take your word. So long, Belle. Take good care o' Betsy."

"I will, I will!" she promised. "Hurry now!" she added as a heavy boot hit the bottom of the stairs. She stood there, her face pale, her hands clasped to her breast, staring at him in a way that caused his heart to catch.

Harve pulled away, went silently but swiftly down the dark hallway and descended by the front stairs. The lobby of the hotel was not crowded, but the few men there paid him no attention. He reached the bottom of the stairs and headed back toward the rear, looking for an outside door.

He found a small storeroom in the rear with a door letting out on the back. He slid out the two-by-four bar and stood it on end and eased the door open.

His heart leaped. The black was standing tied to the buckboard wheel. He didn't see anyone near.

Harve had his pistol ready as he stepped through the door. Walking upright, he dropped the pistol against his leg, heading for the horse in as casual a manner as he could muster. He almost reached the animal when he heard the gut-wrenching shout.

"There he is!"

The black danced with excitement as Harve jerked at the reins. A rider came thundering down the alley. As the horse danced with excitement, Harve finally jerked the reins loose. He hit the horse with his hat, moving the animal into the path of the hard-riding horseman and ran for the barn door. The horse Squint was riding—Harve had a momentary glimpse of the wild face, the upraised gun—breasted into him and he felt himself flying through the air. He landed on his hands and knees in the hay litter and scrambled ahead into the protection of the barn.

The ladder to the hayloft was there and he took it, his legs pumping him up. Outside he heard Carney bawl: "Crick and Spade, get around back, quick! He went in th' barn!"

"He ain't goin' nowhere," Crick Justan raged.

Harve was up in the hay now, moving toward the front of the barn. There was a big opening there through which the hay was brought into the loft. There was a rope and a pulley which was used for hoisting. He edged his head out the opening, saw Squint and Dingus right below him, waiting for the others to get into position. The rope used for hoisting hay swung away into the darkness, the loose end secured at the corner of the barn. He edged over there, stooping as the roof slanted in until he came to the small opening, from which a workman directed the operation when it was in use. He squatted and while he worked, he heard a racket on Main Street as people began filing curiously back to see what all the fuss was about.

He got the rope untied and pulled in all the slack. When it was taut, he tested it, muttering a little prayer that it was firmly secured. He squeezed himself through the opening, wrapped the rope around both hands and jumped, letting himself fall at the end of the rope like a pendulum. He went through the air with his boots aimed like a battering ram. His steel-studded bootheels caught Squint full in the vest and knocked out his breath and swept him out of the saddle. Dingus yelled in fear and a gun blasted in Harve's face a moment before he catapulted into Dingus.

Harve untangled his hands from the rope and ran for the black, which was circling, trying to rid itself of the ground anchored reins.

He grabbed the reins and swung up, his heels drumming against the sleek black side and the horse leaped away, almost leaving him behind. He gripped the barrel with his legs and dug his fingers into the flying mane. People scattered as the black, whistling shrilly, thundered down the alley. Then the horse snorted and slid to such a quick stop that Harve went up on the heaving neck. The entire alley was blocked with more men and horses than he could count.

"Just sit tight there, son, and nobody'll get hurt," Marshall Bill Pelley said. Without turning his head, he gave orders in a quiet voice. "Four—five you fellers go and round them up at the barn."

Pelley had control of his men—they filed past Harve, riding quietly without looking at him. In a moment, he heard the terse command as they took Squint and Dingus, with others of the posse circling the barn to corral those remaining.

"I was fixin' to give myself up, anyway," Harve said in a dull voice.

"Was you now, son?" Pelley asked in a kindly voice.

"Go on, lock me up," Harve said in a ragged voice. "Put me in jail. Guess that's where I belong."

Pelley dismounted. "First things first, Harvey."

A tall, old man with a gray spade beard got off his horse to stand beside Pelley. "This the boy who took my niece?"

Pelley shook his head. "Didn't exactly take her, Wendel. She lit out after him. Guess she'd heard about your place."

"Do you have to carry on about that part of it?" Wendel Morrow asked in a pettish voice.

Men roughly pushed Dingus and Squint forward. "Got two, Marshal."

The two men looked stupidly at Harve.

"Take 'em over to the hoosegow," Pelley directed and then, Crick Justan and Spade Cooley were herded down the alley. "I guess that does it."

"There's one more," Harve said in a tight voice. "Wes Carney is up in Belle's room right now."

Pelley was striding away toward the back door. He halted when the door flew open and, in the dim light, Wes Carney pushed Belle out ahead of him. He held her close to his body, shielding him, and waved his pistol.

"Don't move a muscle or so help me, I'll kill her!"

"Nobody's movin' a finger," Pelley said in a quiet voice. "You better drop your gun, Carney. You can't get away."

"The hell I can't! Just make a move an' I'll shoot!"

He moved out, holding Belle close to him and began inching along the wall, backing toward the barn. Everyone was quiet, watching in fascination at the drama being played out.

Carney stopped, obviously trying to make up his mind. He said, "All you fellers, line up against the wall with your back t' me." His voice was taut, the sound of a desperate man.

"Do what he says," Pelley ordered and walked across the alley to stand with his face to the wall. Others moved slowly in obedience to Carney's tough words. All but Harve. He took advantage of the darkness and diversion to slip out of the alley.

He ran on his toes down the walk in front of the hotel and ducked into the first through passage beyond. He raced down the narrow space between two buildings and emerged in the rear of the hotel and turned right, still running. He could hear Carney cursing somewhere beyond, in the darkness. He slowed, edging toward the corner of the building and, when he reached it, Carney backed right into him.

Harve swung the pistol with an unaccustomed fury controlling him. The downward sweep of the heavy pistol crumpled Carney without a sound. Harve caught Belle as she was falling with Carney.

The men lined against the wall surged toward them with a mighty shout.

At the first light they all gathered in Pelley's office, a motley lot. Harve watched Wendel Morrow tugging at his gray beard, happy that the man had agreed Betsy couldn't be moved. She'd regained consciousness and Doc Spicer was cheerfully optimistic about her quick recovery.

Looking sideways at Pelley, Morrow said, "I figure that by the time she's able to travel, I can have a place ready for her. The Sykes' place is available an' I'm goin' to take it up."

Pelley nodded, looking at Harve. "New neighbors, Harve. Old man Racker's ready to turn the Double H over to you. He wants to know if he can stay on. He's an old, old man and it'd be a pity to turn him out."

Harve nodded, feeling self-conscious under the eyes of those present. Out in the jail a commotion set up as Carney and his gang began squabbling again about who was responsible for what. Sighing, Pelley went to quiet them.

Morrow spoke to Harve: "I was a bounty hunter for a long spell, Harve. Most o' them fellows out there are wanted, with a price on their head. Guess you got a right smart wad comin'."

"I don't want it," Harve said.

Belle came in quietly, drawing the scarf off her head. She looked at Harve and said, "You can go see Betsy now. She's awake and asking for you." She saw Pelley coming from the cell and she wondered how much more she should tell him. *Just wait,* she told herself, *and see what happens. I'll be around to watch.*

Harve lost all his indecision as he headed for the hotel. He went at a fast walk, thinking joyously that the Sykes' place was close enough to Double H for him to ride over any old time. He whistled as he walked, a little tune about moonlight, roses and a pretty girl.

The three of them, Pelley, Morrow and Belle watched through the window of the marshal's office.

"That kid has purely been through hell," Morrow observed.

Pelley nodded. "An' now comes the time when we all got to talk turkey." He swung around and faced Belle. "How much you gonna tell him?" he asked. "That kid saved my life an' I'm gonna save him all the hurt I can."

Belle glanced at him and her lips trembled but she said nothing. Pelley took her hands very gently in his own. "Belle, them boys out there, 'specially Wes Carney, been singin' like jaybirds. I know who you are and I wanna know what you gonna tell Harve. Like Wendel says, he's been through hell . . ."

"I'm not going to tell him anything," she whispered. "I just want to watch and see he's all right . . ."

"Good," Pelley said gruffly. "Wendel had to make a decision, too. He got rid o' that house up in Jemez Springs, or he's goin' to . . ."

"Already done it," Morrow said with an impatient wave of his hand. "When me and my boys joined up with you . . . well, you let me know I couldn't have my own niece long as things were like they were."

"Old man Racker spilled his insides. Wants to make things right with Harve. Just think, it all started with Hack Holley tryin' to do right by Harve." He looked at first one then the other. "Guess it ain't such a bad old world after all."

Wendel stroked his beard. "Always heard a zebra don't change its stripes, but if that kid can come through hell without gettin' burnt, guess there's hope for even me."

"Amen," said Marshal Bill Pelley.